The Last Message

Fernando Armas Pérez

The Last Message
Fernando Armas Pérez
www.fernandoarmas.com

Original title: *El último mensaje*
Translated by Fernando Armas

Printed in Spain
Legal Deposit TF458-2023
ISBN: 9798395487285

Printed by GRAFIEXPRESS
Calle Álvarez de Lugo 51
Santa Cruz de Tenerife 38004
Spain
922236930
info@grafiexpress.com
www.grafiexpress.com

Layout, design and production
Copyright © 2023 Fernando Armas Pérez
All rights reserved

Partial or total reproduction of this work by any means or procedure, including photocopying and computer processing, and the distribution of copies of this edition through rental or public lending, are strictly prohibited without the written authorization of the copyright holders, under the penalties established by law.

The Last Message

Fernando Armas Pérez

Speciem decipit mundus

(*The world deceives with its appearance*)

I

The wet and desolate street rested in silence while the black sky wept upon it. The winter days of Sylvanville drove away pedestrians shortly after four in the afternoon, as soon as the weak sun disappeared over a hazy horizon. The water sparkled around the bright yellow street lamps, and the hedges along the sidewalk swayed, battered by the relentless cold and dense wind descending from the peaks of the Peakshire Range mountains. Below them lay the valley where the city was nestled.

Sylvan's Corner, a bar-café and restaurant, was one of the few establishments that had remained unaffected by the ups and downs of the country's economy. Michael adored it because it evoked his youth, when it truly had a much cozier atmosphere, despite offering customers a poor selection of drinks and three or four regional dishes. Authentic local food from the valley, though.

It was named so because it was built at the intersection of White Oak Avenue and Cedar Lane over sixty years ago. Michael spent many afternoons there with his friends and Anne, enjoying the view of elms and cedars through the large windows. Those were the evenings they would chat animatedly, filled with laughter and youthful emotions. Conversations where they shared academic concerns, the results of the latest exam, or the most recent gossip about teachers.

At Sylvan's Corner, time seemed to stand still.

Some things had indeed changed. Thirty years ago, when customers entered the establishment, they were greeted by the smell of freshly brewed coffee and a rustic decor with exposed brick walls that created a sense of warmth and comfort. It was only logical that three decades later, they would have had to make changes. Old Bob had passed away long ago; his children sold the bar and moved to the coast in search of a milder climate to pursue other businesses focused on surf tourism.

The new owners made some refurbishments to adapt to modern times: they covered the bricks and lightened up the space, they replaced the wooden bar with a sturdier one, and added new tables and comfortable chairs, perfect for relaxing and enjoying coffee.

After a quick look at the menu, he noticed that the drink options included more variety than Bob had ever considered, from classic *espresso* to flavoured or imported coffee.

The food also offered other dishes, but the new owners did not neglect that important part of the local spirit of Sylvan's, "fortunately," thought Michael. The café offered a variety of breakfast and lunch options, such as sandwiches, salads, and fresh pastries. The menu proudly highlighted that the ingredients they used to cook were fresh and of high quality, and that many of them were local products, provided by valley farmers directly from their fields to the kitchen of Sylvan's. At least, that's what the luminous sign placed at the entrance of the place said.

He browsed on the menu and was happy to discover that they had kept Anne's favourite salad, so she wouldn't have to rack his brain to suggest something.

He also couldn't complain about the staff. He missed Bob, of course, a friendly and talkative guy. When he entered the café that afternoon, he looked at the employees with nostalgic eyes and missed the close and friendly treatment that Bob gave to his customers, whom he knew inside and out.

These girls, hired by the current owners, were also friendly and helpful, he could not complain, but no one shouted his name cheerfully from the other side of the bar, as Bob used to do since he popped his head out. Bob used to ask, "As usual, Mike?"

The extreme winter weather in Sylvanville woke him up from his memories; another lightning bolt, which illuminated the sky, brought him back to the present.

For Michael, it was going to be a terrible winter afternoon, one of those he avoided describing in his novels. But even so, he looked through the wide window of Sylvan's Corner with writer's eyes, trying to capture the essence contained in every drop of the rain, every cold gust of air, and every flash in the sky. He felt comfortable, protected, and excited about the meeting in the warmth of the place.

He looked at the ceiling and figured in his head, "How long has it been since we last saw each other, Anne?" He rehearsed the question like so many other pieces of sentences that rushed through his head, because he did not want to run out of ideas and topics when she arrived.

He saw his reflection in the glass of the window and laughed at himself. "You're not young anymore, Michael. You're not young anymore," he scolded himself, shaking his head as if he were talking to his past self, the young Michael Whitmore, a college student and inseparable companion of Anne.

Anne would have also changed after decades without seeing each other, that was obvious, although in the photos that headed the articles of the Daily Beacon where she worked, she differed little from the tender twenty-year-old girl he flirted for some time.

"How long?"

The question hung in the air; the vibration of his phone interrupted his memories once again. It was her.

"I'm running late due to traffic. The taxi driver says we'll be there in about five minutes."

He looked at his watch and replied with a simple "ok." Immediately, he realized he should have been more polite and tried to type out a message with his thumbs. "What the hell should I say?" he asked himself, but he gave up on writing anything more and looked at his reflection in the window, which was fogged up from the warmth of the cafe. He shook his head again.

The door of the café opened and a gust of cold air made him shiver. He decided to change seats. Surely, Anne would prefer it too, and he remembered her wrapped in her winter jacket crossing the college, so delicate and sensitive that he would surround her with his arm to warm her up until they reached the car park.

He sat in the new seat facing the door to see her come in. And he returned to his memories. Surely reliving their youthful love would make them feel young again. "Are you sure?" He shuddered with doubts and trembled like a big teenager. "You're being immature, Michael," he scolded his reflected self in the window.

A waitress approached and interrupted his imaginary conversation. She took out her guest check pad, but he didn't let her ask the question.

"I'm waiting for someone. I don't think it'll be long," he smiled and looked at his phone again. "On the way!"

He raised his hand to get the same waitress's attention, and apologized for making her come back as she had just left, and asked for the menu. He hoped to surprise Anne with some different food. He quickly glanced at the dishes, but he doubted if her tastes had changed. "I don't think so, Michael," he said to himself, "you haven't changed much either," and decided on the salmon salad.

"Two salads and a bottle of fruity white wine, please."

The waitress took note and turned around just as another gust of cold air blew in with Anne as she entered Sylvan's Corner. She unwrapped her scarf and unbuttoned her winter jacket. Then she looked around the place to locate him, and he quickly stood up to make himself noticed, waving his hand and smiling with childish enthusiasm.

She responded with another big, natural smile that reassured him. She advanced with determined steps through the aisle, and they hugged tightly, long, and sincerely, like true friends who have always loved each other, regardless of the passage of time.

"Amazing! Miss Harrington, you haven't changed a bit. You look even better than in that photo in your newspaper."

Anne didn't blush like she used to when she was shyer and more introverted, and it bothered her to be called a "nerd." She pulled away, pinched his cheeks as she used to do when they met, and Michael's heart beat excitedly with the memory of Anne's cold hands. It was as if, suddenly, they both went back to the moment when their lives separated to build the future.

"You haven't changed at all either, Mike. You still have the same stupid look on your face and curious eyes."

They laughed and Anne's friendly insults caused the knot that had been gripping Michael before seeing her, embracing her, and smelling her to unravel. The trip back in time was fast with just two harsh adjectives as fuel.

Everything was back to how it always was.

Michael helped her take off her coat and they sat facing each other, and she started talking just as she used to, rushing through the information with a million issues, and he just listened captivated, with a renewed heart and a silly grin he couldn't control.

The waitress brought a tray with napkins, two glasses, and cutlery of better quality than Bob's. She reached out, placed the tray on the bar, and took the *Fruits of the Sun* wine bottle, uncorked it, and filled half a glass for Anne.

"I hope you like it. It's white, fruity, and grown in our valley," explained Michael, waiting for her to smell and taste it.

"Excellent!" exclaimed Anne, and when they were both served, they toasted to old times.

"To the past and the reunion, Mike!"

"To the present and the future as well, Anne!"

The first hour passed between food, conversation, sips of wine, and toasts to friends, family, and Sylvanville.

"So, have you come to pry into the intimacy of our town, Anne?" Michael asked her.

"I think we're both here for the same reason. According to your last message, you wanted ideas for your new novel, right? Tell me something!"

"No. Not at all. You're a reporter, and you'll copy me," he joked. "It's more of the same stuff. You know I like crime, investigation, psychological thriller, blah, blah, blah."

"So much information! I'll publish it tomorrow, Mike. The whole country will know! You're always so tight-lipped about your projects. That hasn't changed," she protested.

"Okay. After publishing *Three Widows*, I've been going through a rough patch," he confessed.

"But you had success... didn't you?" she asked.

"To a certain extent. You know how Crimemaster Publishing works. Maybe I made the mistake of agreeing to be chosen by the best publishing house for the type of books I'm best at".

"You have the advantage that all the readers you write for buy Crimemaster's books, haven't you?"

"Exactly. It was very tempting. They sell more, but you also sacrifice profits. And you know that books have their peak and their decline. If you stop, you miss the train."

"I thought you were fully satisfied. I've read so many press reviews, and the critics of Three Widows placed you in such a good position. I thought you'd be ecstatic and that you had made a profit. Personally, I think you created a great work. I loved the plot! You had a great idea, and I'm sure it will make it to the movies. I see it having the potential to become a screenplay. You can't complain," she encouraged him.

"I hope so, and that Hollywood has ears in this old place," she crossed her fingers with both hands. Then she took the glass and they toasted. "To Hollywood, cheers!"

"So, let's focus on the issue that brings us back to the valley," Anne resumed the conversation.

"Do you know anything about the murders?" Michael asked.

"If I had more information, I wouldn't have come home. They sent me because I was born and raised in Sylvanville, my city."

"Ours... Our city," Michael corrected her.

"Okay, our city", she accepted the amendment. "Is Sam still in the police?", she wondered.

"Sam passed away two years ago."

"No way? What happened to him? Was he killed?

"Nope! it wasn't the job; it was an impossible cancer. You know he smoked a lot and over the years he stopped taking care of himself. Some mates told me he drank too much too. You wouldn't believe how much weight he gained. Such is life! Michael regretted.

"What a shame! He was a great guy, concerned about the community. He got involved in all the university groups," she smiled, noticing Michael's mischievous grin. "I know what you're thinking," she added.

"Hey! Don't look at me like that. If you're insinuating that Sam chased after every skirt, that's your thing," Michael retorted.

"You're the one who just mentioned it," Anne reproached him. "But you're right. He flirted with everyone. Nevertheless, he was a good guy. The other thing is just instinct."

The two of them fell silent and looked at each other. Anne rubbed the window with her sweater sleeve, made a circle, and looked through it.

"Things haven't changed that much here. Two or three streets spruced up and some buildings refurbished. Otherwise, it seems to be the same as the postcards Ed used to sell in the Bridge Road shop.

"Do you mean the ones we used to steal when Ed wasn't looking?"

"Hey! Finish the story, Mr. Writer. Admit that it was you who *distracted* him."

Michael laughed at the memory of the two of them running down the avenue sidewalk as if Ed had discovered them and was furiously chasing after them.

"But we did some very creative things with them. At least they were put to good use," said Anne.

"True. It was fascinating to invent those stories. Do you remember any of them?"

"Actually, no," she replied, looking up at the ceiling, trying to recall a memory.

"I'll never forget the one about the river..." Michael tried to give her a hint.

"That's right! You started by saying that we went fishing one spring day. Something like that, wasn't it?"

"Perfect. And then what happened was that we got our hook and line tangled up in a corpse floating downstream," he continued.

"I realized on that same day your brilliant capacity for mystery storytelling. I was absorbed as you recreated the story of the corpse and how it ended up in the river. I couldn't resist adding this story in the report I did about you," she said.

"And I was thrilled to read it. Let's admit that there was also a reporter pushing hard inside you. I remember the satisfaction on the English teacher's face when she read your publications in the college newspaper," Michael praised her.

They smiled at each other for a moment that was interrupted by the doorbell and another gust of cold night air. It took a while to close, as someone in an electric wheelchair tried to manoeuvre past the umbrella stand. An elderly person slowly walked down the aisle towards their table.

He stopped and asked the waitress something, and she pointed to the back of the café. The man moved slowly and stopped again when he reached Anne and Michael's table.

"Excuse me, sir," he addressed Michael, "would you mind opening the restroom door for me?"

Michael nodded and got up obligingly. The man turned his wheelchair around and got up with difficulty. Anne also helped him.

"Thank you very much, miss... From now on, I will have to go on my own," he smiled wryly.

Michael, however, accompanied him to the same restroom door, waited for him to enter, closed it behind him, and returned to his seat. He sat down again and was silent for a moment. Anne knew, by his downcast expression, what he was thinking, but she let him reflect and express himself:

"It's a shame to reach that age without companionship, don't you think?"

She blushed for the first time all evening and looked at him with the eyes of memory, of the moment of farewell, of what could have been a love story. Did they ever love each other as lovers or was it the perfect friendship between a man and a woman?

At that time, she felt comforted and comfortable in the small-town atmosphere of her hometown, but there also arose the almost inevitable need to prosper, to pursue a dream: to write and become a reporter and travel the world in search of a unique report, or rather, "the" report, her own report. With luck, she had had more than one, and Anne placed herself in the top positions of famous American reporters.

They were young and the impulse of youth pushed her to emigrate to a big city. She did not underestimate her family's hometown or her school, high school, or university. The streets, squares, and avenues of Sylvanville were so familiar to them that she adored that reunion because those homely places comforted her and made her feel safe. Anne used to boast about her city to her colleagues in the newsroom, arguing that there was no other place as beautiful as her valley.

"What are you thinking about?" Michael asked her.

She came out of her memories and answered him:

"I think that I am very happy to meet you again in our Sylvanville's shelter and that I am glad to see that nothing has changed between us despite the years." She reached out the hand and Michael gently squeezed it.

The bathroom door interrupted them again. The man in the wheelchair returned with short and indecisive steps, so Michael hurried to help him.

"You're a gentleman," the old man flattered him. "Mister...?"

"Whitmore. But you can call me Michael."

"The same Michael Whitmore? *Three Widows's author*?" he asked in astonishment.

"Yes, sir. The same one. I hope that if you have read the book, you liked it." He didn't interpret whether the expression of perplexity meant a positive or negative judgment of his book.

"Of course! I have a copy at home that I never get tired of reading. It would be fantastic if you could sign it for me. I don't live far from here. If you want to, you can come with me, and in a moment..."

"I apologize, sir..." Michael interrupted him.

"Silverman, Oliver Silverman", he introduced himself.

Michael shook his hand and apologized again, "I'll be spending some weeks here, and I think my friend and I will have dinner at this place several times. I'll leave you my card, and we can meet another time. How does that sound? I'll be delighted to sign *Three Widows* and discuss it with you".

"Of course, of course... Forgive me, and excuse my presumptions. You must be very entertained for a poor, disabled old man to come and bother you. I repeat my apologies, Mr. Whitmore."

"It's no trouble. But call me Michael," he insisted. "Believe me, my girlfriend has an important work commitment, and I have to take her home immediately."

Anne looked at him with a furrowed brow. Why did he have to lie and use her as justification? Regarding that issue, Mike hadn't changed either.

"Then, Miss. I beg your pardon too. Thank you very much. You've been lovely. Don't ever change."

"Thank you, Mr. Silverman. Have a nice evening," Anne replied warmly.

The old man walked slowly back to the door, excusing himself to the customers to let him go on. The waitress opened the door for him and bid him a fond farewell.

"So, I have an important appointment?! You haven't changed a bit."

"Yes, I have," he disagreed and pointed to the grey hair at the temples. They've lost colour.

"You such a fool!"

"All right. I was just an excuse. We may never see Mr. Silverman again," he smiled. "Let's return to the issue we are here for. Are you sure you don't know anything?" Michael insisted.

"I've already told you. The police have no evidence, no reason, no witnesses. Whoever's behind it is a cunning guy."

"Just all I need for my new novel! A slippery, clever killer who leaves no trace. Well, that's just it. We'll just have to keep asking awkward questions of the mayor and the police."

"That's my job, Mike," she stated, snapping her fingers to encourage him.

"You'll keep me informed and let me help you, won't you?" he asked.

"Of course, I will, silly boy. You'll have material for your book, and a good material. Besides, if we don't find out anything, we'll invent it, and if I don't get my Pulitzer, we'll get your Book Award, at least."

She held out her hand to close the deal. Michael took it, brought his lips to hers, and kissed it gently.

"Miss Harrington, it's a deal. It will be a pleasure to work with you," he talked softly.

Michael called the waitress and asked for the bill.

"Shall we have breakfast together tomorrow," he asked Anne as they left.

"I'll see you at dinner. I've got some appointments at the town hall and I'm hoping to get some more information."

"Yes, that's a good idea. That's a good idea. I'll be out on the streets, too, keeping my eyes wide open," he said and widened his eyes.

"Silly boy," she reacted while Michael was helping her to put on the heavy coat.

"Anne is still cold," he thought.

II

For Mr. Silverman, it was an ideal night. Unlike Michael Whitmore's opinions about winter in his novels, the cold, snow, and storms brought him calm. Over time, he learned to enjoy the beauty and serenity that comes with the icy wind and long nights, as it shaped the ideal conditions to snuggle up in a warm coat and enjoy a hot tea while watching the snow falling gently. Winter was an opportunity for thinking of his life and the important issues in his life.

He arrived at the entrance of the house and closed his umbrella. He entered and took the lift to the second floor. When he reached the apartment, he left the chair in the corner of the small hallway and walked into the bedroom.

The telescope had been discreetly pointing at Hilda's house for several weeks. He sat down and looked through the eyepiece. There were no signs of the neighbour. No one in the neighbourhood had noticed her disappearance, except for himself: Oliver Silverman.

The fog drifted down the street and the humidity fogged up the bedroom window. Silverman stopped staring at the house when it became impossible due to the poor visibility.

He took off his warm flannel shirt, hung it on a hanger, and headed to the bathroom. He looked at himself in the mirror and ran his hand over the scarred skin that extended over his back and shoulders. He felt nothing, no pain at all. The fire had erased the nerve endings, and time had healed the physical pain he used to suffer. At that point, his skin didn't hurt anymore, but his heart did. He smiled. Someday the world would compensate him.

"Karma? Is that what it's called, Adeline? Karma. Cosmic balance?" He approached the mirror, as if he wanted to tell it a secret and whispered: "Oliver, a person's actions in this life can influence their future destiny. All actions have consequences. Isn't that right, Adeline? And if you do good, you reap good, and if you do evil, you'll face the devil!"

He sat on the bed, picked up his smartphone, and typed a message slowly. He sent it, then turned it off and plugged it into the charger on the bedside table.

He wrapped himself up and dedicated a thought to Michael Whitmore. How lucky he was to have met him at Sylvan's Corner! He would have never imagined shaking hands with his favourite writer. He was euphoric.

"Mr. Whitmore," he addressed Michael as if he was sitting at the foot of the bed, "you had a brilliant idea. I loved *Three Widows*. Maybe you've come to meet your past. Okay, I'll address you informally, Michael. Have you come to meet your past?"

And he fell asleep to the lull of the wind and the patter of raindrops on the skylight.

III

The mayor stood up as soon as Anne entered the office. He belonged to a younger generation than her. Anne had left Sylvanville long before the mayor Edwin Thorne finished his law degree. She knew he joined the Conservative Party, flirted with politics and took less important positions, and at the end, he came to rule the town.

"Miss Anne!" he exclaimed and walked to meet her. He shook her hand and asked her politely to sit down. "Feel at home here, please. Would you like something to drink, a tea, some water?"

"Very kind of you, Mr. Thorne. I had breakfast before coming to the town hall."

"You're a legend. Let me thank you again for contributing to the greatness of our town. Your report on *Three Widows* and Michael Whitmore was a great boost for the valley and Sylvanville."

"Thank you very much, Mr. Thorne. I spoke from the heart and the roots that bind me to this land. It was a wonderful experience, and whenever I can, I make some reference to my home town, of course. It's not just my job..."

"I know. It's your passion," he interrupted excitedly. "But please, call me Edwin. Can I call you Anne?" he asked as he walked around the massive wooden desk and sat in the costly armchair that towered over his shoulders and head. The journalist thought he had chosen the chair on purpose to convey authority and power.

"Of course, Edwin." Politicians did not intimidate her. In fact, nothing scared Anne Harrington. She had spoken with the President of the United States on several occasions and with several Vatican officials, as well as with rebel leaders in conflict-ridden countries. Edwin was just a regular citizen of the valley. He knew the peculiarities of the people of Sylvanville inside out.

Anne sensed why Thorne had won the last election by such a large margin compared to the other candidates. Mayor Edwin Thorne commanded respect, and she had been told that he was admired in his community. His joviality and dignified bearing gave him a presence that also inspired confidence and respect in her. Therefore, she treated him with respect.

Despite his youth, Thorne had gained experience since he was a college student and had since developed a distinguished career in public service and held some important positions in the town before becoming mayor.

"I've been told that you are investigating the loss of those elders in our city. We don't have much information, but the police are trying to make clear what has happened and we believe we are getting closer to the perpetrator," he said bluntly, as if he was in a hurry because there were many issues to deal with.

"I have no doubt about it, Edwin. I've already been informed of your ability to resolve conflicts and your skill in uniting the community around common goals," Anne had excellent skills to tease the information she wanted. She put all her effort into emphasizing who she worked for: "The Daily Beacon, as you know, has sent me because I was born and raised in Sylvanville, and we're trying to help in the best way the town considers is the best for our important journal," she highlighted *important*.

"I really appreciate the warm comment and offer, Anne. There is any doubt, yours is one of the most significant newspapers in our country. And I must admit that it's a privilege to have a citizen of Sylvanville among its top reporters," the mayor returned the compliment tactfully. "It's the police recommendation not to provide information until the chief suggests it. We communicate with the prosecutor every day... But I promise you that any news we need to be known The Daily Beacon will be the first to know. Not only have you made a good impression on me, but you're also a model citizen. For Sylvanville, it's a pride that you've achieved such an important position in a national newspaper," he repeated the praise.

Anne knew politicians' demagoguery perfectly well, saying one thing but doing another, and thought Edwin could be a tough nut to crack. Thorne was a persuasive speaker and had a charismatic way of connecting with people. "A professional politician," she thought. But she didn't give up.

"Don't worry," she insisted, "You have my word that any information you provide me today, from the prosecutor's office or from the police, will not reach the press without your consent and without you reading it first. I am the first to defend the interests of Sylvanville, as you can imagine," she concluded and placed her hand on her heart to try to gain his trust.

The mayor hesitated for a while and replied: "Well, there's not much I can tell you. Actually, there's nothing," he admitted, "except a small number of assumptions. The victims have no connection to each other. We don't see any motives for killing them. Nothing has been stolen from the houses where the bodies were found."

"They're all older people. That's a starting point, don't you think?" She explained.

"Sure. It's the only thing that links them. But it makes us think that it's someone cowardly who is looking for easy victims because they are elderly and don't have the strength to defend themselves. That means the suspect could be a man or a woman, young or old... In other words, over eighty percent of this town could be the killer! Do you understand?"

"I do. The figures of suspects are almost one hundred fifty thousand people, aren't they?" She estimated accordingly to the current population of Sylvanville.

There was a short silence and then she spoke: "I'm not going to subtract the time you have spent on me, Edwin, and allow me to reiterate my gratitude for facilitating the interview with the police chief."

"No problem, Anne. Call me at any time if you find something. I'm sure your talent for investigation will come to conclusions that can help us in this issue."

Thorne escorted her to the door and said goodbye with another warm and friendly handshake.

IV

In the morning, Oliver Silverman woke up to the dim and cold winter light. The curtains were open, revealing the same grey morning as the day before. He didn't mind. The small apartment was located on the second floor of number 11 Evergreen Lane. Perhaps the name was given because of the rows of trees that in Spring were filled with lush green leaves.

He had looked for a residential and quiet neighbourhood, with a nearby park he could walk to with Musca, the Golden Retriever he had found abandoned and so, he had adopted. Unfortunately, he had to put her down years ago due to the terrible canine disease that affected her hips and hindquarters.

He had rented the apartment just over a year ago and it was part of a comfortable two-story building, facing the west side and with a good view of the other houses.

His way of interacting with the neighbours evolved as months and years passed. Now he emulated James Stewart, in the style of Alfred Hitchcock, and spent long hours watching them with his eyes on the fishing bobber, like a fisherman who patiently waits for a fish to bite the hook.

When he arrived on that street, he developed another way of *sneaking* in their lives, as he used to say. He let himself be invited for coffee or tea with pastries, until they revealed the necessary information to him.

With Hilda, the woman across the street, he had spent long afternoons and weekends. A well-directed conversation, with the right questions, allowed him to get to know her completely: the distant and close family, the grandchildren and school, the nephews finishing their studies, the disagreements with former work colleagues, the secrets of her ex-boss, the finances...

He became very fond of her and close friends and they spent hours and hours together, but that stage ended when Hilda's health got worse and she repeated the same topics constantly, so he gradually stopped meeting her.

The outbreak of the virus and the terrible lockdown, which condemned the population to isolate themselves from each other, was the perfect excuse.

During the lockdown time, he developed a habit that kept him in touch with the street. He bought a telescope and some good quality binoculars on Amazon and began to spy on his neighbours' lives through the lenses. Silverman became less sociable, more introverted and silent, as he was afraid of getting infected and dying alone in that apartment.

He became a reserved man, who used to observe the street and conjecture about the Evergreen neighbourhood and started attending to all kinds of movement from the window...and that was a great challenge that kept his mind awake.

Analysing the neighbours' behaviours through body language, expressions, routines, and speculating about the progress of their lives became a pastime for him. All of this helped him keep his brain busy, so he could concentrate, anticipate, and enjoy his solitude.

The window was a screen of the street with which he interacted. Like others did with their smartphones, computers, or PlayStations, the old man had his own entertainment. He thought those gadgets were cold, bare, and detached from the pure existence of the souls that inhabited the street. His neighbours were not images created by computers, but real flesh-and-blood people with true emotions.

His own reality show.

V

This time, Mike was late. When he arrived, Anne was waiting for him at the table reserved in the Rustic Hearth, a contemporary restaurant that offered WiFi to its customers, *with a cosy avant-garde decoration*, according to the reviews that Anne found on Google.

Michael had been told that he could enjoy typical dishes from Sylvanville. A local flavour in a rural, yet modern and warm atmosphere.

"It's your turn to order, Anne," he said after a warm hug and sitting across from her.

"Okay. But I'll let you choose the wine... I'm going for roasted chicken with grilled vegetables. It's my grandmother's recipe," she decided.

"Accepted, grandma's recipe! Your mother also cooked it very well. I remember having this dish on some occasion."

"That's right. She used to make it on Sundays. It wasn't as good as grandma's, but I admit it was tasty."

They fell silent again. Each one remembering the story from their perspective and at the same time, imagining what the other felt in the past. Michael broke the silence and suddenly changed the subject:

"Tell me more about the conversation with Edwin. Through WhatsApp, you barely sketched an idea," Michael requested.

"I think you don't have many arguments for your plot at the moment. Unless you want to make up the killer. There are one hundred and eighty thousand possible suspects. Not to mention if it's someone who came from abroad to the city."

"Wow. Good for the killer."

"And, as you mentioned WhatsApp: did you send me a message by mistake, Mike?" She picked up the phone and turned it so that he could read the screen.

"No. Why do you ask?"

"Look at my phone." She passed it to him.

Michael whispered silently, looked at her perplexed, blushed with anger, and re-read the question quietly, "Do you remember what happened that fateful day?!," he exclaimed with astonishment. "But who the hell knows anything about that?"

"Lower your voice," she begged him. Murmuring with raised eyebrows, she approached Michael slowly and whispered: "did you tell anyone?"

"Absolutely not. Are you crazy?!" Michael defended himself. He didn't expect her to question he has always been a faithful friend, so he responded quickly without thinking, "And I understand that you didn't either."

"Of course not!" Anne looked at him with apologetic eyes and stretched out her hand. They both held onto each other to support each other. Words weren't necessary if they had their hands together. They knew each other well enough not to say anything that would erode their relationship.

The waiter approached with a cart carrying two steaming plates. There was a tense silence as he placed them on the table. They waited for him to move far enough away to continue their conversation.

"Thirty years! Thirty years?"

"Yes, Mike. It worries me. But also, who has my phone number and why are they sending this message now?"

"It could also be a mistake. Don't you think? It has happened to me on occasion that I receive a call or a message from strangers. One wrong number is enough," he tried to calm her. "Who is it from?"

"It's a hidden number or a business one." She showed him the phone screen again so that he could see that there was no information on the contact's profile. "There's no name of the user of the line."

"The police," said Michael. "We can talk to the police chief. I'm sure they have resources to find out the source."

"To be a writer, you seem a little foolish. Should we tell the police what happened?" Anne questioned him.

Michael looked at her in silence and knew what she was feeling at that moment.

Despite the fact that the years had buried the incident, the scenes remained engraved on the retinas of two frightened young people who fled and sought refuge in silence, in letting time go, and in forgetfulness.

Anne thought that perhaps the anxiety, fear, and stress of being discovered also weighed in her decision to leave Sylvanville, and she was afraid that a ghost from the past would push her out of the town where she grew up again.

Meanwhile, Michael carried the guilt of his past self. An impulsive, carefree, naive, and quite immature boy. He did flee the town. It was a forced exit. Could he continue his literature career at Sylvanville State University? Of course. He had already won writing awards in some local and state competitions. He obtained excellent grades, and his professors encouraged him to take the leap to the general public. However, he left to start from scratch as a news writer for local newspapers, as a writer of intriguing stories that he presented to some contest, or as a scriptwriter for some series. Gradually, his role as a novelist displaced the scriptwriter and columnist, and he made a name for himself in the field of fiction genre, with exciting and chilling works such as *The silent witness* or *The puppet master*, until *Crimemaster Publishing* aimed at him and published *Three widows*. His masterpiece sent him to world stardom. His successful book had already been translated into several languages.

By that time, they were young, although they had no excuses. They were also of legal age and criminally responsible, and they should have fulfilled their duties as citizens. They should have helped the victims.

But as the years went by, Anne and Michael lost their fear of facing legal consequences and covered up the remorse of having committed a serious crime due to their lack of responsibility and empathy.

Did the message come by mistake? Michael looked at Anne with concern, and he was sure it couldn't be any other way. How could a message appear from so far in the past?

Analysing Anne's eyes, he knew she felt remorse for making a selfish decision when they were more concerned about the impact on their reputation in a not-so-large city and the success that their family and professors predicted for them after their fruitful lives as students, a success that was opening doors for them, and they were afraid those doors would close if they were blamed and the news spread around the town.

Michael came up with a response to reassure her and insisted that it was a mistake.

"You're right, Mike. I think it's just a mistake. Let's not dwell on it."

Anne put the phone face down on the table, and they resumed the evening chatting about trivial topics. At the end of dinner, they said their goodbyes with a warm hug before heading home.

VI

Mister Silverman couldn't believe that no neighbour or relative had missed Hilda so far. The house had been empty for a week, and the newspapers thrown by the freckled teenage delivery boy, who raced down the street on his bike every morning, were piled up messily in front of the house's entrance.

He was waiting for a reaction from her family, but no one had shown up. He was saddened by Hilda's loneliness. How could it be that no one called or checked on her to see what was wrong? He thought he might have to call the police himself... But it wasn't his responsibility, and he didn't feel like explaining his curious habit. "If nobody cares about our old lives, why the hell do I have to explain anything to anyone?" he thought at that moment with some outrage and went back to his tasks.

Hilda was the responsibility of the town, her acquaintances, friends, and relatives. His heavy burden was already enough. He never managed to overcome the loss of Adeline and all the projects they had carefully crafted together. They couldn't have children, so they devoted themselves to each other. Oliver Silverman was born to die with Adeline. And so it happened. When she left forever, she also took his soul with her.

He settled into the comfortable wicker chair he had outfitted with plush cushions for watching his favourite reality show in the afternoons, when an unexpected movement on Evergreen Street caught his attention. He didn't use the telescope but the binoculars, which allowed him to be more agile. That boy was new to the neighbourhood. He saw him trying to force the front door and when he wasn't able to, he stopped, looked in both directions of the road, and looked straight ahead to his window. Silverman's heart jumped in his chest because he thought he had been discovered; however, the translucid window had kept his privacy, and he smiled.

"Don't you see me, boy?"

The guy jumped over the garden fence and broke into the house.

That break-in at Hilda's house upset him. He approached the dresser in his room and took the notepad and a pen. On the other hand, he was happy that there was finally some news that would allow him to break out of his routine. When there were changes in the usual Evergreen scene, life took on some shape, and he could better cope with the painful wounds of the past.

He spent the whole afternoon setting up the telescope to point at different rooms in his neighbour's house and kept note-taking in his pad. When daylight disappeared completely, he sat at the kitchen table, placed Adeline's silverware in front of him, then took the soup and told her the news. "There's a strange boy in Hilda's house, honey," and explained her his plans.

He finished. He stood up, cleared the table, and gave Adeline a kiss.

"And I love you more, my dear," he whispered.

He washed up and before going to bed, he picked up his cell phone and typed a message slowly.

He leaned his head to the side to observe Hilda's house and fell deeply asleep.

VII

It was half past nine at night. Anne didn't hear the message or feel the vibration of her cell phone as she dried herself off after a relaxing bath. She didn't remember seeing the shower salts that she usually bought in Sylvanville, so she took advantage of her stay in the city where she was born to buy a couple of packages. The unique rose fragrance and granulated texture were unmistakable, so she stretched out in the bathtub and rubbed her body until she was in ecstasy. No one would hear her moan with the bathroom door closed.

It had been an unproductive day. The mayor was right. The information provided by the police was practically the same. There were no suspects, no motive, and aside from the age of the two deceased, there was no connection between them.

She wriggled in front of the full-length mirror. Despite her age, Anne had an enviable figure. She struck flirtatious poses like a teenager. She rubbed a moisturizing cream scented with a similar aroma to the bath salts. Her body shone for a while until it absorbed the product, leaving her skin soft and smooth. She caressed herself again and had a fleeting thought of Michael, which she immediately pushed aside. Then she rushed to the bed, unfolded her pyjama, and put it on.

She picked up her cell phone. The small number twenty-three on the WhatsApp application made her click her tongue. "What a pesky boss I have."

She knew she didn't have to read or answer any messages outside of working hours, which were very strict for journalists or reporters like her. Nevertheless, she clicked on the icon, and one of the messages caught her attention, without a number.

"Have you and Michael remembered that fateful day yet?"

Anxiety caused a pressure in the pit of her stomach that spread to her chest, and she saw her skin prickle. She tapped the screen to access the phone app, but her trembling hand opened the browser by mistake. She dropped the cell phone on the mattress and took a deep breath, as her therapist recommended. After a few seconds, she returned to the bed and managed to contact Michael.

"Michael?" He responded with a smooth voice, trying to joke, but she hurried him: "I'm serious. You have to come right now!"

"What's going on, Anne? You're worrying me."

"I just forwarded you the message. Please, read it. Come immediately. I'm scared," she begged.

The night streets of Sylvanville barely had any traffic in the early morning, and it took Michael no more than five minutes to reach Anne's building. He lived in a modest one-bedroom apartment on Hemingway Road, in the expanding southern area of the town. It was a development distributed in perfect blocks, with buildings no higher than three floors. Michael sold the house where he grew up, as it was too large for him. With the money from the sale, he bought the apartment, and invested in a new car, and in the production of his books. He chose that place because all the streets, parks, and squares had names of American writers such as Emily Dickinson Road, Tennessee Williams Boulevard, and Walt Whitman Park, perhaps with the illusion that someday, some mayor would also put his name on a street, and he himself would be part of the eminent American history.

He parked near the entrance, and as soon as he pressed the intercom, Anne opened the door. When he arrived at the apartment, she hugged him and let some tears fall on his shoulder. Michael felt Anne trembling, and it wasn't from the cold. On the contrary, she seemed to be burning with fever. He remembered that she blushed before taking an exam at college, and her body reacted with heat when she was nervous. He tried to calm her down.

"Come on! Lie down on the couch." He carried her over. "I'll make you some tea. Do you still like black tea? Tell me where to find it."

"Yes. Open the second door of the kitchen cabinet, starting from the right."

Michael lit the fire and let the water boil. He added a spoonful of tea leaves and waited a couple of minutes.

"What a smell! It takes me back to the afternoons we spent studying, and your mother would bring us a cup," he was trying to distract her from her worries by talking about trivial topics, like how the tea in Sylvanville wasn't like it used to be, and how, in general, vegetables didn't taste the same anymore.

"Agriculture and genetics are worsening the natural taste of things. You know, Anne?"

"I published a report about that. I don't know if you ever read it," she replied, calmer.

When the tea arrived, she sat up, held the cup with both hands, inhaled and exhaled, took a sip, and exhaled.

"Do you feel better?"

"A bit better. But I can't stop thinking about it. Who's sending me these messages? Why now? How is it possible that they have my personal phone?"

"Let's take it step by step. Let's analyse it calmly and decide what steps to take. It's like a chess game. Do you remember?"

When they were students, Anne and Michael played endless games of chess. She was the one who proposed it, telling him that it would improve their analytical and concentration skills, and, as they both loved writing, chess would also help them be more creative, or at least, that was what Anne used to argue.

"Of course, I remember," she replied. Michael was right: they needed to use their cognitive skills to approach the matter and not to let the emotions control their minds. "Which piece should we move?", asked Anne.

"I think we should make a pawn move. Let's leave our king and queen to rest for now. I would simply ask who he is and how we can help him," he proposed.

"Agree. it's a simple and cautious step. Should I reply now?"

"I will do it for you. It's late. Let him not sleep," he said and he reached for the phone.

She approached the kitchen table. Michael observed her from behind. Her silk violet pyjamas fit naturally on her body, not as thin as when she was twenty, but well-preserved. Anne regularly went to the gym and he envied that time had not treated him the same way.

"You have a magnificent body, Anne. It seems like the years have improved it."

She smiled at him.

"Nearly, but thanks for appreciating it. I assure you that I have invested money and mental and physical effort. Otherwise, I wouldn't be able to maintain my sanity with work." Now she was more relaxed. "Do you want me to write it?"

"No. I insist. Let me have the device and I'll take care of it," he whispered the message as he typed. "Dear 'whoever', I'm sorry to inform you that I lack information regarding the story you're asking about. But, if you need any explanation, please be more explicit. Of course, I would be delighted to meet with you and discuss your concerns... Best regards."

"What do you mean by meeting?! Are you crazy?!" Anne raised her eyebrows and opened her arms.

"Let me see. Of course, you wouldn't go to that meeting, if you decide to accept the proposal, of course. We would both go. We've moved a knight and to approach the king surreptitiously."

"He might not even respond," she doubted.

"He will or she will."

"Why are you so sure?"

"Because this person wants something from us. Maybe justice, maybe money."

"Well, justice doesn't benefit us at this point in our careers. Can you imagine what my boss would say if he found out? When you work at the top, the fall is more painful. The media is politicized and our rivals would take advantage of any scandal to undermine our foundations, to question the ethics of our workers."

"I know. But the effect can also be the opposite. A conflicting story can have a lot of circulation and also catches the reader's attention for spin-offs, prequels, sequels..."

"I don't like the sensationalism. The press that seeks blood, pain, and misfortune to make money... It's not my style."

"I know that too, Anne. But in this game, we have to be prepared for the next move and walk in another's shoes. We might even be obliged to sacrifice the queen to win the game."

"Hey! Then you have to become the queen! I won't. I like my life and I enjoy my job. I like my present, with its ups and downs. It seems unfair that an event from thirty years ago should intrude in the best years of maturity. I've been attending a therapist since then and I've tried my best to overcome the past." She almost cried. "And I have paid a lot...

"You're right. We don't know how the story ended for those involved. We read the news in Sylvan's papers, but we continued with our lives," said Michael.

"We were kids," she regretted.

Michael understood that she wanted to move on, just as they did the day the local media reported the accident. He felt the same way. Youth was a stage of development and maturation, in which their brains made emotional decisions without having reached full development. And like all their peers, they too were impulsive, intense, and fluctuating.

"Well, now we're not those young students. We've learned to control our whims and make decisions based on thinking, haven't we?"

Anne nodded silently; she was calmer after half an hour of conversation and two teas. Michael suggested turning off their phones, forgetting technology, and enjoying each other's company, as they did in high school and college. He set an example by turning off his phone and leaving it on the small dining table. Then he took hers, and noticed that two small green ticks indicated that the message had been delivered to the recipient, but kept it to himself. He simply pressed the switch-off button and looked at her satisfied.

"Stay," she begged, holding his hand.

"Are you sure? Do you want me to sleep here, on the sofa?"

"No. Come with me." She got up and grabbed his hands and she gently pulled him along.

They lay down. She curled up on the bed on her side, Michael wrapped his arms around her, and slipped his hand under her pyjamas and caressed her smooth, fragrant, and moisturized skin. He reached her chest and knew, as it used to be, that they both desired each other.

He leaned his head to the side to observe Hilda's house and fell deeply asleep.

VIII

Mr. Silverman cleared the breakfast table and left the plate and cutlery in the sink. It was early and the weather seemed to be about to give a break. The sun was rising somewhere behind the buildings on Evergreen Lane. He looked at his watch and calculated that soon a ray of light would flood the bedroom and prevent him from observing the street clearly.

He "connected" with the neighbourhood throughout the *Rear Window* to see what morning movements were taking place in Hilda's house.

He watched the boy go back and forth, as if he had settled in despite not being an owner. He alternated between binoculars and a telescope and tried to shape an idea that he wrote down in his notebook.

Anne and Michael were also awakened by the bright light filtering through the bedroom blind.

"Good morning, Mike. Did you sleep well?"

"I did. It was a good sleep night's sleep!" he exclaimed, stretching and yawning. "It's been years since I slept so well. I've forced this lump of flesh that carries me back and forth for hours and hours of sleepless nights."

"Well, stop writing at night. It's easy, isn't it?", she criticised him.

"I'd wish. But my muses visit me at night, like the park's felines and owls, they usually appear very late, when there's silence and darkness. Maybe I attract them more at that time!" he joked.

"You are a fool! That's what you are, an arrogant fool. You're the one who calls them at those hours to justify sleeping in the morning."

"Lately, I haven't been able to sleep in the mornings either. I'm not as lazy as I was when I was twenty, Anne. I've grown up!" he complained.

"Well, prove you're mature by making coffee and preparing some toast."

"Hey! Cunning as a fox!" He gave her a kiss and went into the bathroom. "A quick shower, Anne, and I'll prepare breakfast for you!"

She replied with an "okay" and couldn't resist checking if the person had responded to the message from the night before. She picked up the phone and went back to bed, thinking it would be better to be lying down, just in case.

"He read the message, Mike!" she shouted to overcome the noise and splashing of the shower.

"What? Wait until I come out."

Anne grew impatient and went into the bathroom.

"I said he read the message, but he didn't respond. It's marked as 'seen'. I don't know what worries me more, the silence, the text he sent us, or what he'll reply."

"Maybe that person didn't expect a move from you. Maybe he's analysing the game or sleeping," he managed to distract her.

Anne headed to the kitchen and started preparing breakfast. Michael came out wrapped in a towel.

"It was my turn, remember?"

"But waiting makes me anxious. At least this way helps me to forget," she replied and continued beating eggs. She placed some strips of bacon on the griddle.

Mike dried himself off while observing the urban landscape from the window and noticed that Sylvanville's sky was giving them a splendid day.

"Do you feel like a walk in the park? That way we can see the improvements our mayor made," he suggested.

"And shall we run along the paths for a while?" she asked, pulling back the shower curtain.

"I prefer to walk. 'Running is for cowards.' Haven't you heard that?"

"Every passing hour you become more foolish."

Michael smiled and set the table for breakfast. He no longer felt capable of enduring more than five minutes of jogging. The work of writing kept him sitting in front of the computer for endless hours almost every day.

The city council recovered many native forestry species that had been cut down over the centuries to build the first colonial town and created a perfect place to escape the hustle and bustle of the noisy Sylvanville's rush hours. The designers of the town hall made an effort to conceive a place with a relaxed and peaceful atmosphere and divided it into recreational zones, so there were areas for ball sports, others for picnicking equipped with rustic oak tables and benches, places to make a fire and enjoy an outdoor lunch surrounded by nature.

They put the emphases on families and distributed playgrounds throughout several areas. They not only repaired old swings and slides, but also created new spaces for skating and added interactive playing elements for the little ones.

They recovered the walking paths and separated pedestrians and bicycles by a lane for each. Since its opening, the park had become an important meeting point for the citizens of Sylvanville: they used to come to exercise and take in fresh air by walking along the paths that ran parallel to the Mountain Brook River.

Michael parked his Chevrolet Spark in the spacious parking lot at the main entrance of the park. He got out and ran to open the passenger door for Anne.

"Wow. Some habits die hard."

"It's silly. In these times, people would look at me with disbelief. I'm afraid they might even call a 'looney bin' to have my head checked."

Anne stepped out and took a few steps back.

"I like that you bought a simple car model, Mike."

Michael knew she was saying it sincerely and without any intention of rubbing anything in his face. But he was a little annoyed.

"In our country, success is measured by possessions, but I thought it was better to be valued for my work and not my possessions. Don't you think?" he commented seriously.

"I don't know why you're upset. I completely agree with you, and the Spark is a compact vehicle with efficient performance. It's very practical for this city."

He responded with a simple "let's go" and they walked hand in hand for a few meters. Anne had a feeling based on Michael's attitude. She knew him well enough for these reactions not to go unnoticed. Not only did she know him, but she had a special ability to sense the emotions of her interviewees after years as a reporter and journalist.

Perhaps Michael was hiding a disappointment and didn't want to discuss it with her. She remembered about the small percentage he received from the sale of his works and how all books have a peak of readership that slowly declines over time. His writer friend had been silent for months, not participating in forums. Where were his income coming from? Was he going through a rough patch? she wondered.

"What are you thinking about, Anne?" The question interrupted her thoughts.

She hesitated to answer, brought her hands to her mouth and exhaled to try to warm them. She concluded that it was not a good time to bring up that matter. What if she was wrong?

"I'm still thinking about those two messages and their intentions," she responded.

"So many years have passed. Everything would be prescribed. There's nothing to fear. We'll play this game. If we look at the positive side, I could get an idea for another work and you would be able to get 'the' report."

Michael's phone rang.

"Michael Whitmore speaking," he answered.

"Mr. Whitmore, excuse me for interrupting. I don't know if you remember me. I'm Oliver Silverman. We met at the Sylvan's Corner. You were very kind and gave me your phone number to meet up and sign my copy of *Three Widows*. Perhaps I've been too bold..."

"Oh! Of course, I remember you," he interrupted Mr. Silverman. "And I'll be happy to meet up. We can schedule it right now. Does that work for you?"

"It brings me great joy, Mr. Whitmore. I'll consider myself a privileged reader. Tell me when it's convenient for you. I have the availability of a retiree who sleeps little. So, any time is good for me, regardless of the day or night, so tell me what time would be the best for you," he insisted.

"How about tomorrow morning?"

"Oh! Great! Mr. Whitmore. If you'd like to have breakfast with us, we'd be happy to prepare your favourite dish. I suppose it's the one you mention so much in your work, am I right?"

"Good intuition. I appreciate your invitation. Is ten am okay?"

Silverman accepted the hour; still he would have accepted three am. Any visit to his lonely home would have made him happy. He could say it was a first-time event, as no one had entered that home in years.

Anne looked at him as if asking who it was. It seemed that Michael had regained his enthusiasm.

"Nothing important. A publisher wants to propose better publishing conditions and even consider turning the text into a screenplay," he lied.

IX

Silverman left his mobile phone on the bedside table after the conversation. He was excited but also feared that Whitmore had accepted the visit out of obligation and might not show up the next day.

He picked up *Three Widows* from the shelf and placed it on the bedside table. He would try to read it for the fifth time to refresh his ideas before the author arrived. *Three widows* had something in common in their lives. Whitmore's plot, a mysterious murder case in which three close neighbours and friends were involved, clinging to their friendship to overcome the loss of their husbands. The police focused on them, but they could not gather evidence beyond having a hunch. However, Whitmore would reveal dark secrets about each of the women, including past tumultuous relationships, financial problems, and commercial and personal connections between the three husbands, suggesting that the murder was carefully planned.

For their part, the three widows joined forces and threw red herrings to convince investigators that they had nothing to do with the murders and divert attention from themselves. The thriller gradually intensified as they tried to identify the real killer, while the pressure from expert criminologists gradually closed in on them.

The story, full of unexpected twists and turns, kept Silverman guessing about what the murders hid, and the magnificent final closure did not leave critics indifferent.

No one questioned the mastery of the plot and the author's descriptions of the town. When it became a bestseller, Sylvanville elevated Michael Whitmore, and the town (that saw him born and raised) began to appear in many national media, which attracted curious readers to discover the settings in a 'literary tour' promoted by the publisher and the town hall.

Anne wrote a very comprehensive report with details about Sylvanville that she knew perfectly and a biographical review of the author with whom she shared so much for many years.

Oliver Silverman sat in front of the window again and looked through the binoculars. That young man in Hilda's house bothered him. He nicknamed him 'the nephew', to say something as he didn't know his name. Was he a squatter? He estimated that the age was around thirty. In the last three days since he arrived, he had not accidentally crossed paths with him, although the old man tried to force an encounter when he went out for bread and the newspaper every morning. He tried to vary the hours and go out more frequently. He felt the need to pry into the guy's private life. But he was a rather nocturnal young man. "Maybe he has an evening or night job," he thought at first, and after several days without progress, he felt annoyed by his presence. He was going to give him a lot of work, and he didn't have that much time.

X

They began their walk by taking the path flanked by a dense canopy of oak trees that projected towards the sky, forming a natural tunnel. In the summer, it acted as a parasol, creating a cool and shaded atmosphere. Now, the two of them would surely prefer fewer tree canopies and more sun to mitigate the low temperature. The town hall kept the path clean and free of weeds so that sporty citizens could run without danger.

Birds chirped from high branches. Michael looked up to try to distinguish them. Near the Little Creek Bridge, the oaks opened up on the river side, which flowed parallel and revealed the landscape of the other bank, large stretches of crops and pasture.

"We'll cross the 'Lovers' Bridge'," Michael suggested to try to get to the opposite bank with more sun.

"Lovers' Bridge. Who came up with that name?" Anne referred to the moment when the students of their generation renamed it. They used to sneak to the other side and take refuge in the abandoned farm to have relationships, away from the control of the tongues of Sylvanville. It was an old building with over a hundred years of history and belonged to the Perth family. Rumours of ghost stories circulated: creaking boards, as if some ancestor of the former residents had stayed in the barn to finish the farm work. Although Michael always maintained that they were school rumours, perhaps started by the teachers themselves to prevent students from skipping classes and meeting secretly in the place.

"I think it was Sheila. Do you remember her? Red-haired and very freckled.", he answered.

"Right. She was dating Samuel, wasn't she? And they went to the farm almost daily," she reminded with a little chuckle.

They both laughed with a mutual understanding between them. They had also come to the farm on occasion. Anne stopped in the middle of the wooden and rock bridge.

"You always used to stop here," Michael reminded her too.

"Exactly. The view and sound of the water is overwhelming, isn't it?"

Michael surrounded her with his arms and kissed her. She held his head and let herself be carried away. But another chuckle stopped them.

"What are you laughing at?" Michael asked, holding her by the shoulders, his brow furrowed.

"It's a mix of joy and memories. With that kiss, I took a trip back in time, and memories of us and the high school kids rushed over me," she explained.

Michael smiled, kissed her forehead again, and took her hand. As they left the bridge, they continued walking in the opposite direction of the river's current.

"I hope you have a lot of luck with tomorrow's interview, Mike. I think you deserve much more."

Michael didn't respond. He tried not to look at her so she wouldn't notice his look of unease. His career as a writer seemed to be hitting rock bottom at the same time as his bank account. The book *Three Widows* was a turning point for him. He couldn't come up with a better idea that surpassed or equalled *Three Widows*, and he couldn't afford to publish another story of worse quality. The level of success overwhelmed him. He felt he had jumped very high, but that it was a temporary thing and he had put a ceiling on himself. The terror of failure kept him away from the laptop keyboard, which he carried with him across the country, and also away from the "idea's book," as he called the notebook that was part of his hand luggage whenever he travelled. Flying above the clouds inspired him, he had declared in some interviews.

"Do I sense you're feeling down? Is something wrong?" Anne asked. For her, Michael was an open book. She knew him too well not to know that that grimace meant he was worried.

"I have to admit that I'm worried about the low productivity of my current work," he confessed.

She stopped him and pulled his hand to lead him to a solitary wooden bench that faced west.

"So, the lack of inspiration is more serious than what you told me. Is that it?"

"To a large extent, it is. As the saying goes, 'where there's a will, there's a way'. But I've been stuck for months on dozens of beginnings that don't go anywhere, because *Three Widows* gets in the way."

"Have you thought about the possibility of creating a spin-off of one of your characters? For example, you could turn the detective into a Poirot and make a series."

"Yes, of course. I've tried. Prequels, sequels and spin-off stories."

"What about going back to teaching and dedicating yourself to it like you did at the beginning? What do you think of the idea? That way you could take a step back and see your work from another point of view."

"I've considered that too. But what kind of students will I have? Disruptive adolescents who only care about their personal image? How do you teach and convey the value of the rich literature of our country?"

"You'll have to deal with that. You can't have a class tailored to your needs."

"I don't need a tailored class, but I do need measures for the classes. Everything is too lax, Anne. The students have their food made, served, chewed, swallowed and digested for them. The teacher's role is that of a caretaker. I don't want to be the school's 'parking attendant'."

They both fell silent and the sound of the trees swaying in the wind became more present.

Anne wasn't expecting the revelation and she was worried about her friend's emotional state. Mike had always been a locomotive and not a freight wagon, let alone the last wagon. The matter seemed serious. She already had two problems on her hands: how to get some information about the two murders and how to solve the anonymous messages that brought danger from their past to their careers. And Mike?

XI

Silverman was a finicky, methodical man with predictable routines. He woke up early with mixed feelings; on the one hand, he would have the author of his favourite book, Michael Whitmore, in his home, but on the other hand, he was afraid of being disappointed in case he didn't show up and didn't want to insist on contacting him again. He gave himself a positive response: "maybe Michael Whitmore will find a gap in his schedule for another day," thought and went to the kitchen.

He tried to have breakfast, setting two places as usual, and after clearing the table, he returned to the bedroom to concentrate on Hilda's house. A task that would keep him busy while waiting for the writer's visit.

His neighbours were predictable and routine-oriented, they had perfect repetitive lives, and that made his work easier. However, he had not been able to establish rules for that secretive young man, and that worried him. Nothing could be out of his control.

He stretched his arms over his head and reviewed his notes again. "He hasn't had visitors; he doesn't usually make big purchases; he sleeps and wakes up at different times; he eats without any pattern; he can be on the TV or the computer at any time. His life is... random?" He wrote the word and question mark down in his notebook.

Despite the ups and downs, the old man was happy with the challenge. Sneaking into the life of the young squatter was his second priority, a kind of revenge for entering the neighbourhood, forcing Hilda's door, and settling without anyone's permission.

Within his field of vision, he noticed the figure of a man in a trench coat approaching his building. He got up from his chair to see what he was doing in front of the main gate when the intercom rang, and he jumped for joy.

"Do Oliver Silverman live here? My name is Michael Whitmore."

The old man's heart raced with excitement, and he stuttered in response, like a child who adored Santa Claus and sat on his knee to take the souvenir photo of that Christmas.

He pressed the button to open the gate and ran to his apartment entrance door.

Michael didn't have time to press the doorbell as Silverman was waiting for him behind the peephole and opened it immediately.

"Mr. Whitmore! It's an honour to have you in this modest dwelling. Please, I would be honoured if you came in and felt at home."

"It's a pleasure to meet a reader. I don't always get feedback on my works, and for me, the information readers can provide is just as important as what I write for them," he stated, while Oliver helped him with his coat, as if he were his butler.

"Please come into the kitchen and take a seat," said Oliver. He pulled out one of the chairs and Michael assumed the other was for him, but Silverman stopped him from sitting in it, indicating that he should sit in the one he had pulled out. "No, please sit here. I have that seat reserved. Tea or coffee?"

"I think coffee would be better. Maybe it will clear my mind," Michael replied. Oliver brought over a steaming cup of coffee and they sipped in silence.

"I'm surprised, Mr. Silverman, that you walk so magnificently well. The other day at the bar, I thought..."

"Please, call me Oliver," he interrupted Michael and asked: "Do you mean the electric chair?"

Michael nodded and Oliver replied: "I consider it more of a psychological tool than a real need. Sometimes my joints get stiff and I can't move forward. I have difficulty with the peripheral vein circulation in my legs, and I can't walk long distances. Adeline is very insistent and makes me use it every time I walk around Evergreen."

"Is Adeline your wife or daughter?"

"Adeline is much more than my wife. We've known each other since we were young, as our parents were both servicemen and both families were neighbours, you know, family-style housing on base where officials used to live. And we fell in love when we were thirteen."

"Long term relationship! What a beautiful story! Do you mind if I take some notes? I'm going crazy looking for ideas for my latest novel."

"Of course. But you won't have much to tell from my life. I barely have any friends or visitors. If it weren't for Adeline, I would be alone."

"And where is she?"

"She sleeps a lot. You know, the ailments of the elderly. But don't worry, I'll tell you everything I can learn from you. Excuse me, I'll be right back with the book in just a second," he said, walking decisively to the bedroom, leaving Michael puzzled. The difficulty he had at Sylvan's Corner didn't seem fake to him. Now he questioned it.

He came back right away with the book, smiling like a child with a new toy. He carried the book with the cover facing him. It was a simple job by the publisher, but intriguing. A dark background and three female silhouettes stood out more than the title in large white letters. A red stamp indicated that it was the second edition and reflected the tens of thousands of copies that had been sold. He left it on the table and provided a pen. "Thank you very much, Mr. Whitmore. You have no idea how happy it makes me to have this signature and dedication."

"Thank you for being part of the readers, Oliver. I'd like to know, who your favourite character was."

"I undoubtedly feel a great admiration for Detective Maxwell Chase, from the very name and the perfect portrait you masterfully created. The name was very fitting. A true hound, that Maxwell. Don't you think?" Oliver explained with devotion.

"I agree. I think I started out not giving him as much importance, but his voice grew up until he became the protagonist. Let's say he pulled me along, more than I pulled him," Michael said.

"It's curious how you put it. A fictional character pulls on the hand that creates it. Very curious," Oliver remarked.

"That's right. When I've spent hundreds of hours talking to them, the characters sometimes surpass me, and it seems like they tell in my head what I should say about them. I let myself go," Michael confessed.

"It happens to me too. I understand it perfectly. I've lived with Adeline for so many years that I hear her voice in my head as if it were her own voice speaking to me. But my case is different, of course," Oliver smiled.

"Anyone who dedicates themselves to this world will tell you the same. Characters come to life and sometimes, you can't control them."

"Well, not losing control is extremely important," Silverman pointed his finger at Michael and paused. "Especially on the road and when driving at high speeds with alcohol in your blood."

Michael had a kind of vertigo hearing the old man.

"Did something happen in your life, Oliver? A traffic accident?"

"Oh! Not in my case, but who hasn't had a traffic accident in life, Mr. Whitmore. It's impossible, much less in these times when it seems like life is ending and we have to get to all the activities we do as soon as possible."

"I'm not in that rush," Michael had other arguments. "From my experience and my work, 'haste makes waste', as people usually say."

"Totally agree! Your work is thoughtful and reflective. You have to slow down to move forward later," Oliver said.

"You describe it very well," Michael agreed. "You move forward a little jerkily."

"And what are you writing now, if you'll permit me to ask?" Whitmore asked with curiosity in his eyes.

"Nothing. I have to confess that right now I don't have anything concrete. That's why I take notes. In some corner of someone's life, something may happen that I can turn into a bestseller."

"And what if I confess that I can give you an idea that I believe would be brilliant for your future novel?" The old man, still standing, caught Michael's attention.

"Any thread I can pull on works for me," Michael replied after a brief pause. He was open to Silverman's proposal being useful to him. And that old man had something intriguing about him. Firs of all, his strange disability, inconsistent with the way he moved around the house, and why hadn't he sat in the other chair since Michael entered his home?"

"Follow with me to the bedroom, please and I'll show you something," he said, pointing to the room.

"Won't we wake Adeline?"

"Don't worry. She usually rests in the small living room during the day, where we have the TV set."

Oliver Silverman's bedroom was classic and elegant. It was an almost twenty square meters cosy room with a large wardrobe placed to the right, upon entry, and that gave the impression of plenty of space. In the centre of the wall after the wardrobe there was a double bed. The window, which faced Evergreen Lane, offered a wide view of the trees and beyond.

The old man had a larger-than-usual bedside table with books piled high that caught Oliver's attention. In the opposite corner of the bedside table, there was a desk where Oliver likely sat to read. Michael supposed it, as several wall shelves contained only literature books.

The desk chair preceded a large telescope resting on a sturdy tripod, apparently pointed at a neighbour's house.

Michael had seen the 1954 mystery thriller film *Rear Window* directed by Alfred Hitchcock. Oliver Silverman would be the disabled photographer Jeff, confined to his apartment.

"I imagine you're suspicious of one of your neighbours. Aren't you?" Michael asked, recalling the plot of Hitchcock's film.

"Something like that, something like that," Oliver responded while adjusting the telescope.

Michael began to doubt the sanity of this peculiar reader and admirer. Was he trying to turn Michael into the other character, the police friend? A real-life Maxwell Chase? He knew of cases of readers who turned fiction into reality and emulated the characters by committing the same atrocities that, on paper, had no consequences, but in real life, they did.

"You see, there have been two unsolved murders in this town. Right?"

"Who doesn't know?" Michael asked, downplaying the importance, but a small flame ignited within him.

"Well, I think I have the solution."

"Why haven't you called the police if so?"

Oliver stood up, turned around, and spoke seriously, "Would you come to my house or any other house to clean it, organize it, and fix any damage? Would you buy materials at the hardware store to replenish the forest or fix the town's gardens? Would you repair the railway tracks? Would you divert the Mountain Brook if it threatened to overflow?"

There was no response. Michael understood Oliver meant that it was the police's responsibility to solve the deaths.

He ultimately agreed with Oliver and found it an interesting point of view for a character. He sensed that the old man was resentful towards society. He didn't know information about Oliver's past, but something serious had happened in his life. Did he have a conflict with other human beings? That apartment seemed like a refuge for him and his wife.

Oliver continued speaking:

"I'm glad you agree with me. Now come closer and see for yourself."

Michael observed the poorly maintained garden of the house across the street. In one corner of the porch, someone had made a pile of newspapers and that day's press lay near the front door. It was eleven in the morning and no one had picked them up? He waited for Oliver to give him more information.

"Don't you see it?" He expected Michael to come to some conclusion.

"You've been observing for a time. At first glance, I can tell that the garden is not well maintained, but that the person likes gardening because, in the end, it seems that a lot of time was devoted to it. Time which is not available now. In addition, the pile of newspapers suggests that the owner has been absent for more than a week."

"The owner. "Her name is Hilda Watson. She's a widow."

XII

Anne's voice sounded upset. Michael had turned his smartphone flight mode on, so that no one could bother him during his meeting with Mr. Silverman. It was a habit he had imposed on himself from the first device he bought to the last one, as he considered it foolish to answer a call or attend to the phone while having a conversation, and he was extremely uncomfortable with interruptions.

When he left Oliver's apartment, there were some missed messages and incoming calls from Anne.

"Mike! Where have you been!?" she exclaimed as Michael answered the phone.

"I told you I was visiting Oliver Silverman. Remember?"

"Of course, I remember, but I didn't expect that signing a book could take more than two hours. The person responded to our message. You have to come," she urged him. "Right now."

It was almost noon and traffic was flowing fairly normally, so Michael had decided to walk to the Evergreen neighbourhood because he had woken up early. He now needed a car, and he considered calling a taxi to take him to River Lane, where Anne lived; it would be faster than going back to his apartment.

During the ride, he tried to calm her by sending reassuring messages and announcing a scoop for her search. He believed he had a lead on where to start working and, between the two of them, they would be able to get ahead of the police investigations and even solve the two murders that the detectives had been trying to solve unsuccessfully for weeks.

It seemed as though Anne was waiting for him with her finger on the intercom, as the door opened immediately when he rang the bell.

"Mike! Finally," she said in a faint voice and threw herself at his neck.

"It's ok. Let me know. What's the answer?"

She handed him the phone.

"Thirty million! Thirty?" he read again.

"One million per year would compensate for the terrible loss. He says it will be enough to pay off the debt and that he won't go to the media, the police, or speak to my boss," Anne repeated.

"He has played hard. I'd say he pulled out the queen. He's aiming for a checkmate soon. In a few moves."

"How encouraging you are, Mike! Now I'm really cool," she said, complaining as she walked around erratically in circles.

"Let's see. Not all is lost. First, I'll consult with a colleague. A good lawyer. You might know him. His name is William Archer. He was also at the college by that time, but two years below our grade."

"Archer? I don't know him. But if you trust him, you have my approval. 'In for a penny, in for a pound,' she thought.

Anne sat on the couch. She was afraid of finding herself in this situation at some point in her life. The feeling of guilt had haunted her since she left Sylvanville, and when it intensified, she had to go to therapy.

Now the anguish that paralyzed her was back. An intense and disturbing unease at feeling trapped in a kind of spiral of obsessive thoughts, going over and over again what had happened and shuddering at the helplessness of not being able to change the past.

"I know how you feel, Anne. Often, guilt is a kind of heavy burden that cannot be left behind, and it is affecting you negatively," he said and sat next to her. He hugged her. "You can't let a nightmare defeat you. I'll fix it. I'll fix everything. Do you trust me?"

She looked at him with watery eyes and nodded silently.

"I feel very ashamed, Mike. Sometimes I think I should write my last message in the newspaper or on my social media. Confess and show remorse, free myself from this burden. It's an overwhelming responsibility!"

"Don't do anything. Don't make any decisions right now, Anne." He held her tighter and began to kiss her head and forehead and confessed: "I've also experienced that no one would understand me and I've even felt isolated from society. I've done it myself, to purge my part of the guilt."

"Well, then we deserve punishment"

"It would be disproportionate, Anne. If we had paid for our mistake at that time, I don't think we would have spent more than two years in a state prison. Think about it, at this moment it would be an unjustified punishment and it would ruin our present and our future. Don't you agree?

There was a long silence in which the two swayed embraced on the sofa. Anne was regaining her breath. Mike's presence had always been calming. She would have saved a good amount of money if Mike were closer to her.

She took a couple of deep breaths and the anxiety began to subside slowly. Hope returned thanks to the words of encouragement that Mike's cool head managed to express.

"I admire you, Mike. I don't know how you can be so calm. As if none of this had anything to do with you."

"I have a saying that I usually use when I reach this point of no return. If the problem has a solution, why to worry and if it doesn't have a solution, why to worry?"

She laughed and called him fool, as she had always done since they were young.

"Trust me," he repeated for the umpteenth time. "I'm sure Archer can give me some ideas. I also have an idea myself, but I'll wait until I talk to Willy."

"What have you thought of?"

"Paying him."

"Thirty million dollars! Who do you think you are, Uncle Scrooge!?" she exclaimed in amazement.

"Not at all, ma'am. I have nothing to offer him. Actually, I have only about twenty thousand left in my bank," he confessed.

Anne was surprised by the information. She estimated that Michael Whitmore could have hundreds of thousands of dollars in his bank account after the success of *Three Widows*.

"What happened? Did you start gambling? Betting? Luxury prostitutes?"

"No. None of that. I told you the publisher takes the lion's share and leaves me the crumbs. And they haven't moved the book in a long time. I'm stuck and short on ideas. We talked about this already."

"I know. You told me about your bad luck. But I didn't imagine you didn't have any savings. Anything left after all these years..." Anne stopped. She didn't want to tell him that he didn't have children or a mortgage. Without the main expenses of life, she was surprised that Michael had no savings.

"There's a gap in the information you don't know, Anne. Before the success of *Three Widows*, I survived on minor contest awards and writing for the Sylvann's Chronicle. I did some commissioned scripts...not much else.

"So how were you planning on paying him to keep his mouth shut?"

"Just lure him with money. Set a trap for him. Force him out of hiding and make him show his face. Once we identify him, it will be easier to make our move. Do you understand?"

"Are you suggesting we fake the payment?"

"Exactly. I already used this strategy in my story *A False Poet*. When the villain went after the money, Jack waited for him and exposed him. When he was caught, the game ended in a draw. Neither won, neither lost."

"Of course. But that's fiction. We're dealing with a real case."

"It doesn't matter. Fiction is reality and reality is fiction. Nothing is written, or maybe it is. Everything exists because we create it. Everyone develops different conceptions of reality."

"I understand. We who write can't be sure that the message is ours," added Anne.

"You said it. Your reports come from your sources of research through the resources you provide and the outcome can be reinterpreted. The opinions of readers vary according to education, financial position, sex... Etcetera, etcetera, etcetera."

There was silence.

"How would we do it?" asked Anne with a clear head.

"Are you referring to the trap?"

"Yes."

"How much money can you provide? —asked Michael."

"It would take me some time to explain it to the bank manager, but I think I could contribute one million."

"Wow! You're admirable," exclaimed Michael as he asked for the phone. "I'm going to write to him right now. It's our turn to make a move. Do you agree?"

"Yes. I'm intrigued despite my feeling of guilt. But I need to meet that person and apologize. I have to make up for my mistakes.

"I'd put a bullet between his eyebrows," said Michael coldly.

"Mike! You're not a killer."

"Of course not. But it hurts me to see you hurt," he replied as he began to type. "Dear 'whoever,' I have received your proposal and after analysing it, I have decided to accept the conditions. I think one million dollars per year is a fair amount. But I will pay you the first million dollars and that will obligate you to sign a contract in which both parties commit to keep any harmful information to my interests confidential, and for my part, to report you for blackmail. If you agree, we will set a meeting point where I will deposit the money."

"That's a good move, Mike. Now he will have to come for the money."

"That's what I hope. I'll hide nearby and go armed. I'll take the necessary precautions."

"You mean we'll go," she demanded, pointing her finger at her chest.

"No. Absolutely not. You can't come in case we run into each other. I refuse to risk your life. One death is more than enough."

Anne looked at him with concern. The word "death" filled her with fear. She hugged Mike and nestled under his hero's wings, as if she were a small and defenceless child.

XIII

Silverman shifted in his seat. In just over a week, there were some developments.

"Finally!" he exclaimed the day another young man got out of a taxi, looked both ways down the street, checked his phone, and rang the bell at Hilda's house. He zoomed in on the target, but couldn't see his face.

'The nephew,' the squatter who had broken into Hilda's house, opened the door and greeted him with a handshake. They chatted for a moment before going inside. He offered to carry one of the suitcases, but the newcomer indicated that it wasn't necessary, and they disappeared behind the door.

He inferred that they didn't know each other.

The old man watched them carefully and renewed his enthusiasm by examining the house with the determination to find out who the new person was and why he had come. Was he a relative? Perhaps a squatter friend? He took note of his speculations.

The presence of another person could provide him with more information about 'the nephew,' the most enigmatic character who had ever lived on the street until that moment.

He aimed the monocular at the kitchen where he located them. The nephew offered him a seat and began to prepare tea. The old man scribbled on his notepad what he could read on their lips: "roommate?" he thought he understood. "Internet, computer science, company."

"Voilà!" he thought triumphantly. The few key words were enough to infer the conversation. So much time analysing the neighbours had given him a special sensitivity to deduce things, and with the three words he read on their lips, he speculated on the possibility that the new person wanted to rent a room in a place with good internet connection to develop software. He might possibly be a programming engineer, a computer technician. He sensed that the new person was going to work from home for some internet services company.

He wrote it meticulously and added the questions marks to the statements that he would later have to confirm or refute.

He couldn't afford to make mistakes.

He picked up his cell phone and dialled his favourite writer's number.

"Mr. Whitmore, Oliver on the line. I have news regarding the widow's case," he told him.

XIV

Anne went to the bank branch in Sylvanville the next morning. Up to that point, her walk around her hometown as a reporter had not provided her with any information that could reassure her boss. Now she had to risk seventy-five percent of her hard-earned savings, which had taken years and hours of writing to gather.

As she stood in line, the familiar feeling of anxiety began to invade her, forcing her to pace back and forth and breathe in and out to find balance, the way she had trained with her therapist to try to control her disturbing feelings. Continuous stressful thoughts invaded her, because she was experiencing uncertainty about how to face future expenses, her own security after her working life. What would happen if Michael failed? Many of her financial dreams would also fail or would have to be postponed... forever?

All these thoughts crowded in at once and made her feel overwhelmed by the sensation that the line was not moving at all. She questioned whether Michael's decision was correct with every inch closer to the desk, but when she stopped looking at her ego, the feeling of guilt arose, and she decided to punish herself to expiate it.

"Maybe it's the fair price to pardon my sin," she repeated herself in her mind several times on her way to the office of the director, hoping not to have to talk about financial advice, investments, or the future. She just needed to retrieve one million dollars without giving any explanations. They were her savings.

"I'm sorry I can't dispense that amount of money," the cashier explained. "It's a company policy and it's for our clients' own safety. I hope you understand, Miss Harrington."

Anne tried to control her anger. She was sure that all the customers had noticed her reddening face. She explained that she had been a customer of the institution for decades, had all her capital invested in the bank, and ordered the cashier to let her talk to the branch manager.

"Right away, Miss Harrington," the cashier responded and dialled a number and mumbled something she couldn't hear. "You can go to the director's office," she said and pointed to the door.

The director's office was evidence of the bank's power and status. The Royal Heritage Bank wanted to demonstrate to its clients the strength of the institution, and Anne was familiar with the type of spacious and sumptuous offices like that one. The director seemed like a small figure sitting on a throne in the middle of the office with large windows offering impressive views of the town. The bank spared no expense on furniture and carefully decorated the room for the main employee: a high-quality solid wood table occupied the middle of the room solemnly, and comfortable leather chairs were placed in front for the most notable clients.

Anne felt that so much space was unnecessary and a cost that every client's capital and interest paid for. A luxurious sofa in the corner, even too large for a five-star hotel, was excessive, she thought.

Then all that modern technology, including the huge high-definition screen, was probably for meetings with executives and directors from other branches. Absolutely everything, the artwork on the walls, the tapestry under the sofa, every aesthetic complement was an insult to the effort of earning every penny to impress clients and capture the largest fortunes. In fact, the Royal Heritage Bank was considered the best in the country.

"Miss Harrington, it is an honour to receive you in this modest town," said the director, getting up and walking around the table with long strides to shake her hand and indicate with exaggerated kindness that she should sit down. "Would you like something to drink?"

"Do you have whiskey?" Anne didn't drink alcohol, but she thought that making him spend money on a drink for her would compensate for the irritation caused by so much display.

"Of course. Which one would you like?"

"The most expensive, if you don't mind. The most expensive is always the best," she added.

"Of course. I totally agree with you. What do you think of the Highland Reserve from 1826? It's an excellent Scottish whiskey that is imported directly from Scotland for our offices and our best customers."

"Perfect. I know it. I've tried it countless times during my business trips," she lied arrogantly.

"On the rocks, right?"

"And a little soda, please." The director had to open both bottles.

Anne noticed that the director was an influential and powerful person in the Sylvanville. He must have 'advised' Mayor Thorne, as the opposition parties used to say. It was important to get along with politicians and rulers who, in turn, knew they had to pamper potential campaign financiers.

When Anne finished analysing the director's profile, she concluded that he represented authority and respect from the other bank employees. No doubt about it.

"I've been told you need to withdraw one million dollars from your savings. Know that we are very concerned about our clients' security, which is why the cashier sent you to meet with me," he said tactfully.

Anne thought he cared more about the bank's funds than his clients' security.

"I appreciate your interest in my money, Mr...?" she put emphasis on 'my', and waited for him to complete the sentence.

"Fitzroy. William Fitzroy. Sorry for not introducing myself earlier. But please, I insist that you call me William."

Anne knew the director's name for sure. A huge sign with white letters attached to the entrance door did not go unnoticed.

"Well, Mr. Fitz-fraud..." Anne interrupted, intending to insult the director, but he immediately corrected her.

"Fitz-roy," he said with a grimace, a forced smile.

"Sorry, I meant Fitz-roy," Anne also separated the syllables, mocking the director. "I need to take a million dollars in cash from my money."

Anne was direct and serious. The director didn't know how to persuade her. He estimated that the obligatory question he had to ask would bring him problems. The client was being very insistent.

"You see... ahem! We don't usually dispense that amount of money at once. Surely, you understand that these are strict security measures and protocols that we cannot bypass. What is the purpose of this huge amount?"

"Mr. Fitz-fraud, whose 'million' dollars is it?" Anne insisted, leaning over the massive desk.

"I apologize, Miss Harrington. You precede your reputation, and I know your newspaper is the best in the country. I would dare say the best in the world! I hope you accept half a million dollars today and another half million next week."

"Next week?"

"If you don't mind. They can't give me any more this week, and only exceptionally. I hope you can understand."

Anne began to feel a burning sensation in her neck. She took her phone out of her purse and opened the Whatsapp application, and she typed tremblingly: "Mike, the reckless director says they can only provide me with half a million this week and the other half next week. What do I do?"

Then she looked at the director. "Excuse me, I am consulting with my lawyer. If the proposal is legal, I won't have a problem accepting it, but if it isn't, I will demand a written document with the reasons for non-acceptance and share it with my readers, making a brief comment on this experience."

William Fitzfroy loosened his tie, a clear sign of discomfort. He wasn't worried about a lawsuit, after all, they would win it with certainty due to the large number of lawyers the bank had and because he was sure no client reads the fine print of contracts. After all, when the lawsuit arrives, the client would already have the money at their disposal. He was worried about the name Daily Beacon, the largest daily newspaper read, with millions of readers inside and outside the country, and the majority of them were conservative readers, clients of Royal Heritage, and he was worried about the reputation of well-regarded reporter Harrington.

Fortunately for both the director and the client, Michael Whitmore responded quickly: "Take it. Don't worry, I'll fill in the rest with newspapers. Remember that it's just a lure."

Anne breathed a sigh of relief and felt her pulse return. "Mr. Fitz-fraud, you're in luck. My lawyer says to accept the amount, and there's no legal problem that affects us."

Fitzfroy didn't correct the intentional mispronunciation of his family name on this occasion. He swallowed the parody and his pride to defend the bank (and his position within the institution).

"I'm glad we've reached an agreement, Miss Harrington. I'll be back in a moment with the money. Do you want it in large bills?"

Anne stared at him. Asking Mike another question would raise suspicions, so she resorted to any phrase from any movie.

"Yes, please. Large and unmarked bills." The director laughed at the joke, and both of them relaxed. In just over ten minutes, he reappeared accompanied by a private security guard carrying a bulging bag.

"Do you want to check the amount, please?"

Anne didn't want to stay there any longer. She felt like filling the bathtub, adding salts, and resting while listening to a ballad and drinking a soda.

"No, thanks. I think I can trust you. You're the one who studied accounting, right?"

Fitzfroy smiled vaguely and suggested that the security agent escort her to her car or wherever she considered appropriate.

Anne accepted the offer because she had never ever carried such a large amount of money on her.

XV

Anne's phone woke her up. She looked at the screen, furrowed her brow, and then put on her glasses. It was the boss.

"Ugh! he's gonna kill me," she thought. She sat up and answered: "Hello, Ben. Good morning."

"Well, well. Miss Harrington, how are your holidays going on?"

Benjamin Pierce was a chatty and friendly guy, respected by his employees, but he had untimely mood swings. No one knew when they would happen. But from his tone of voice, the time he called, and the sarcasm, Anne feared that it would be her turn that day.

"Very well, boss. I'm on it. Trust me," she said without giving him any options to extend the conversation.

"What do you mean you're on it, Anne? I haven't seen even a small mention on the last page of our big newspaper. Do you know how much it costs me every day that you don't write anything?"

"I know, Ben. I've been here for many years not to be aware of it," she said on her way to the bathroom. "But I promise you that I'll make it up to you. I want it to be a great story and to withstand the test of time."

"That great story starts today, Anne? Tonight, write the first email with content about the Sylvanville crimes. You have what it takes. I'm sure of it, and I trust you. Okay?"

"Ben, I don't think I can do it today. Give me forty-eight hours, and I'll have something good. Right now, there are only rumours."

"And why do you think you work here?" he asked, and he immediately answered himself: "Because I know you're the best in the world and, therefore, you have more than enough ability to turn a two-word rumour into a full-page article." He didn't let her speak, and concluded, "Contact the photographer and let him help you with the illustrations for your sensational article. Kisses."

"Goodbye, Ben. I'll try..." The editor-in-chief didn't let her finish the sentence, he just finished the call.

Anne put the phone down in a corner of the sink. She looked at herself in the mirror and started to cry. She undressed and got into the bathtub. She let the water run until it reached a temperature of thirty-two degrees. She stayed under the water, as her therapist recommended in stressful situations. The hot water and steam helped her relax her muscles, reduce mental and muscular tension, and provided a feeling of cleanliness and regeneration; a kind of body reset. In that private and quiet space, with the water running over her body, Anne thought that it should be Mike who took the reins of the matter and dedicated himself to writing whatever. She filled herself with energy and was willing to skip her principles, creating a sensationalistic story by making a sort of mix of truths and assumptions, something really attractive that would calm Benjamin Pierce's cravings, at least for a few days. She needed an extension at work to sort out her life... Or rather, to sort out her past.

When she managed to calm down, she got dressed and called Michael.

"Hello, darling," he responded on the other end with the silly, honeyed voice he used for her on the phone.

"How are you, Mike? I'm a mess. I don't have the energy to face all these things. It's too much tension."

"Tell me about it and I'll see how I can please you."

"Benjamin Pierce has just called me with an ultimatum. Can you imagine? Another damn source of pressure that I don't need. He wants me to write something about the murders. What the hell do I say or make up!? No one knows anything."

"I have a solution for you. Do you remember Oliver Silverman, right?"

"Yes. Yesterday, you made the longest signature of your life. I remember."

"Well, he suspects a guy who has sneaked into his neighbour's house. It seems he's a squatter and thinks he may have some connection to the case."

"Really?" Anne asked with a glimmer of hope. "Is it okay if I interview him? Do you think he'll tell me something?"

"Sure, he will. He eats out of my hand. He adores me."

"You're a fool and a silly conceited guy!" she laughed at him. "Okay. I'm interested. Any information can be newsworthy. Do you understand me?"

"Crystal clear, Anne. Shall I come and pick you up, and we plan everything?" Michael suggested.

"Sure. But you'll have to take care of the bait and all that crap... I can't take it anymore. I've had the worst week in a long time."

"Easy girl! You're in the best hands in Sylvanville. Everything will turn out the way we want it to. We are the protagonists and creators of our story, Anne," he said to calm her down.

"Mike!"

"Yes?"

"You're my hero. I love you."

"I'm your knight in shining armour, milady. Don't worry about anything."

XVI

Silverman turned off the TV when Michael called his mobile. He had just left the window for a moment to listen to the news on CNN. Nothing special had happened at Hilda's house that morning.

"Mr. Whitmore, I can't believe it! I am so grateful that you called me. How are you?" Oliver Silverman asked with sincere affection.

"Hello, Oliver. It's a pleasure to talk to you, believe me. You've opened a door to fantasy and fiction with the investigations related to your neighbour."

"I'm so glad to hear that, Mr. Whitmore. If you ever manage to write a novel based on the foundation I've laid, I'll be the happiest reader in the world."

"And you can be sure that you would be my main character," Whitmore promised him warmly.

"Don't make me cry, please. Adeline is looking at me with surprise and disbelief. She knows how important your literature has been in this house."

"Well, then she deserves it even more. I wanted to ask you a favour."

"Of course. Tell me how I can help."

"Do you remember when we met at Sylvan's Corner?" Michael asked.

"Of course. How could I forget? You were so courteous and kind."

"On that day, one of the best reporters from the Daily Beacon, Miss Anne Harrington, was with me."

"Was it Miss Harrington?" Silverman asked incredulously. "I am very lucky that you have helped me."

"For us, it was a huge pleasure. You see, she is investigating the Sylvanville murders. The newspaper is demanding that she send information, but other than your statement, she has nothing that can become news. Would you be so kind as to grant her an interview?"

"That's not a favour. It's a privilege! I have nothing more than eternal gratitude to offer you for this task. Today is a great day, Mr. Whitmore."

"If it suits you and doesn't cause any inconvenience to Adeline, could we meet today?"

"Mr. Whitmore, consider my house as your own. Come when you deem appropriate. We'll be here waiting and it would be an honour if you stayed for dinner."

"Don't worry. I don't want to cause you any trouble. If it's okay with you, we'll bring some low-sugar pastries and you provide the tea."

"It will be a pleasure. We will eagerly await your arrival, Mr. Whitmore, and please insist to Miss Harrington that she considers herself our honoured guest.

It will be a pride for our humble home to have two celebrities from Sylvanville."

Michael had called Oliver from his car parked in front of the apartment building where Anne lived. When the conversation ended, he approached the doorman and waited for him to open the door. He went up happy with the news.

"I have your interview with Oliver Silverman. Let's go right now. We won't take more than ten minutes to get there. Then you'll have plenty of time to write the article, send it to the editorial office, and we can go out to dinner together. What do you think?" he blurted out without letting her intervene at any moment.

"Thanks, Mike. You make everything seem so easy," she said as she adjusted her stockings. Then she indicated the wardrobe with a nod of her head. "The bag is in there."

"Inside, on top, under the clothes?" he asked after opening the two doors.

"Under the pile of clothes. The mess is on purpose, to disguise it," she justified herself.

Michael took the bag and put it on the kitchen table. He opened the zipper and began to take out bills and stack them as he counted the money.

"Wow. I've never counted half a million dollars before. It's quite a lot, isn't it?" She nodded. She went to the mirror and adjusted her clothes by pulling them from one side and the other and Michael said: "I don't think it's necessary for you to withdraw the other amount. I'll fill the bottom of the bag with newspapers. I have a paper cutter at home to cut them to the same size. I'll put the real bank notes on top."

"I haven't received any message yet."

"He'll write, I'm sure. Now he has more than before. I don't think he'll miss the opportunity. I'll leave everything as it was and we'll go to the Silvermans'."

"I'm ready."

The four-kilometre journey crossed the iconic Oak Avenue, a tree-lined boulevard in the centre where pedestrians could walk away from traffic and bordered by bike lanes. Despite the name, not all the trees were oaks. Over the years, they were replaced with other local species that contributed to the creation of a popular space for walking, cycling, or simply enjoying the more urban atmosphere of the valley. Among the Victorian-style buildings, other more modern ones had been built, but they maintained the aesthetics of yesteryear.

Finally, at the intersection with Cedar Lane, Sylvan's Corner appeared.

"Would you like to go back to Sylvan's later?" Michael suggested.

"Well, yes. It's very close to Evergreen. Maybe when we leave Oliver Silverman's apartment, we could stop for coffee."

"I don't think you'll feel like it. With the pastries and abundant provisions... It would be better to come back for dinner time."

Michael parked near the two-story apartment building where the Silvermans lived. Anne liked the cosy atmosphere of the neighbourhood. That was a simple construction in a quiet residential area, better than her four-story apartment block, with double windows, but which did not contain the noise of traffic.

It was made up of four apartments, two each floor, designed to accommodate a small family or couple. The exterior of the building was painted light beige with white details that gave it a clean and modern look.

Anne looked up. Each apartment had large windows with translucent glass. A good choice, as Michael pointed out to her, because Oliver received plenty of natural light and fresh air, but at the same time had an excellent view of the street and the house across the way, which he discreetly pointed to with his thumb to prevent Anne from staring at it.

"Oliver, I'd like to introduce you to Anne Harrington, a reporter from the Daily Beacon," Michael said with great ceremony. He knew the old man would appreciate it.

"Oh my God! What a honour, Miss Harrington! Come in and sit down in the kitchen. I'll make tea right away."

"Here are some cookies. You can put them in the fridge if you like," Michael offered him.

"Oh! Please. Whatever you don't eat today, take it back with you."

"I couldn't accept that, Oliver," said Michael, extending his right hand. "Keep it for yourself and Adeline. By the way, how is she feeling today?"

"Very well, very well. Today she was able to go out with the senior group and do recreational activities. They're very good for keeping her agile and alert. Believe me."

"I'm sorry you couldn't go with her," Anne apologized; she was embarrassed for having separated the beloved couple with her untimely visit.

"Don't worry about it. I never attend those sessions. I have another task that keeps me alert and clear-headed," he confessed, lowering his voice and putting his hand over his mouth, as if there was someone in the apartment who could hear him.

"Yes, Mike… I mean, Mr. Whitmore, told me that you have some important information about the murders of those women."

"That's right. Let me get my notebook. I'm nobody without that little notebook," said Oliver, rushing to the adjacent room.

"But what about the wheelchair?" Anne puzzling whispered. "He's almost capable of running."

Oliver returned right away and didn't have time to warn Michael about the signal for silence.

"Don't worry about my legs. They depend a lot on the distance they have to carry me and the weather," he explained, and continued, "Well, a couple of weeks ago, I noticed that Mrs. Hilda stopped doing her routines."

"Her routines?" asked Anne.

"Each neighbour has a set of routines that are the same every day," he showed her the notebook. "See, for example, Henry Smith gets into his car daily between seven and five and seven fifteen. He returns at eight-thirty. When he parks, he takes the opportunity to water the garden, usually every third day, unless he comes back worried from work. He's a salesman, you know? When he has few sales, he doesn't water the garden. And so on," he concluded and closed the notebook. "I have every personal story collected in fourteen notebooks like this one from the very first day of lockdown until yesterday."

"Wow! You're really methodical. You would make a good journalist," Anne praised him.

"Thank you very much, Miss Harrington. Well, Hilda stopped doing her routines exactly ten days ago. Today is the eleventh. I didn't see her leave the house, so I suspect she's still inside."

"No family has come?" Anne inquired.

"No. Neither friends nor anyone."

"And why haven't you gone to see if she's okay?"

"Well, you see, my Adeline and she had some differences, and I dare not go see what's going on. Besides, I consider that I am not responsible for the life of every citizen in this world. Don't you think?" Oliver said, somewhat irritated, and looked at Whitmore, who nodded slowly.

"You're absolutely right. And what relationship can it have with the other deaths?"

"Well, that Hilda is a widow, like the other two victims."

Anne blushed. Michael knew she was angry and was probably because neither the mayor nor the police chief had given her that information, and an old busybody from a neighbourhood knew it already.

"Oliver. How do you know they're widows?" Michael tried to calm her and continue with the questions.

"Well, because both were neighbours of Evergreen."

Anne became angry again. She felt slighted by the mayor. How is it possible that this information had not come out? She took a deep breath and asked calmly: "Are you sure? I asked the police, and they don't know those two pieces of information."

"I knew the victims, Miss Harrington. When I first came to this neighbourhood, I tried to create a circle of friends and went from house to house. I had good relationships and made some friendships, like with Hilda. But Adeline..."

"You don't have to tell us anything about your private life, Oliver," Michael interrupted. "What do you say if we focus on the facts? On your observations?"

"I think there's a guy who's taken over the house. The first few days, he avoided coming out. Maybe out of fear that some owner might come or because he had enough food stored to avoid having to spend... Who knows if he has any income!"

"Okay. And what have you noticed over the week?" Anne asked.

"I think the guy rented a room to another person. A kind of sublease."

"Really?" exclaimed Michael. "There's your answer for how he's going to make money. A good way to get a property, food, and a small salary for vices. I suppose he consumes drugs."

"No. He's not a drug addict. He drinks some beer, but he doesn't seem troublesome. He even fixed the garden before the other one arrived," he explained. "I nicknamed him 'the tenant.' And I've made a lot of progress in the investigation."

"Your story is intriguing, Mr. Silverman," said Anne, taking a small recorder out of her purse, which she had been using to record the conversation since they began discussing the topic. "Do you mind if I record the conversation? Will it be easier for me to compose my report?"

"Of course, Miss Harrington. Work with your tools. I have my notebook," he smiled. "Let me continue narrating for you... After four days, I still hadn't been able to find out the name of the new tenant. I noted that he settled into the second-floor room with a bathroom. It was easy for me to create a schedule, as the young man had working routines and ate at roughly the same times.

"In the afternoons, he usually strolled or jogged around the neighbourhood. Maybe to the nearby park?" He paused to catch his breath and continued: "Then I realized that the nephew also made some changes."

"Interesting, Oliver. I'm surprised by your method of work. It's admirable," Anne said.

"Thank you very much, Miss Harrington," he put on his glasses and continued commenting on the observations he had made: "Back to the story: that nephew avoided meeting the new tenant. Maybe to give him more privacy? Or did he really bother him?

"My conclusion is that the nephew has that elusive, introverted, and nocturnal character. And, on the other hand, the nephew started going out more frequently at night and on a more regular schedule. I reflected these changes in my notebook," he said and showed Anne the page he was reading.

"Do you suspect him?" Anne asked. "I mean, do you think he could be the killer of the other two women... widows," Anne explained and formulated another hypothesis: "Is it possible that this young man benefits from these women's properties? Keep in mind that they are older, live alone, and are widows. Don't you think maybe they facilitated his entry to feel like someone was visiting and helping them? Do you think it would be a reasonable hypothesis?"

Oliver Silverman looked at her and concluded: "Miss Harrington, I think your hypothesis gains strength. I have the impression that this young man is not as harmless as he appears, and I swear on my ancestors' bones that I will investigate for you day and night under these premises."

Anne had an idea of what she would write that same afternoon, whether it was true or not. Benjamin Pierce, editor-in-chief of the Daily Beacon, would receive a copy of the sensational news he craved in his own mail.

She wasn't in the mood to cling to her principles. Now she urgently needed to finish the report and leave Sylvanville. The same desire that she had when she left to make a career emanated from her heart, a need to rid herself of the weight of guilt that has pursued her. And now, she needed to break with the past more than ever because it was causing her so much anguish that she had to conclude that investigation."

Maybe if she threw out her idea in an advance of the investigations, it would cause a significant stir in the police, and they would call her to refute her arguments. At that moment, she would force them to speak, to tell what they knew. She would get revenge on the mayor and the police chief.

"Please, Mr. Silverman," she said affectionately. "I appreciate this time we've spent together so much. It's enough for me. Focus on Adeline and take a walk around the neighbourhood." Anne was moved by the offer and couldn't resist hugging him.

Oliver Silverman took a deep breath and shed tears of happiness. He had been alone for so long that he was moved by the sincere hug he felt.

Michael hugged him again and praised him:

"I'll seriously consider hiring you as an investigator for my next novel, Oliver. You're a hidden and wasted treasure in this city."

Silverman thanked him for so many compliments with tears in his eyes, which he tried to dry with a perfectly ironed white handkerchief he pulled out of his pants pocket.

"Consider this your home and don't just come when the investigation requires my help. With your permission, Mr. Whitmore, I will send you updates of my observations, and I extend an invitation to my home that you can consider yours," he reiterated.

"We won't disconnect our phones, Oliver. And please, I beg you to call us if you need anything. A trip to the supermarket, accompany you to a medical appointment. Call me whenever you need me."

Oliver Silverman accompanied them to the door with moist eyes. They hugged him again and said goodbye.

Anne and Michael high-fived like two kids as they descended the building's stairs.

"Thank you, Michael. I think we're closer to the end."

"I told you to trust me, didn't I?"

"You're a super sleuth," she said when they got into the car and pinched his cheeks.

"To Sylvan's Corner?"

"No, Michael. I'm going to shape all this information, and I hope to have something for Ben before the newspaper rotary closes. Then I'll let you know where we're going."

"Okay. You're the boss. I'm about to burst with all the pastries I ate," Michael said, rubbing his belly.

"That's because you're a fool."

Both of them laughed.

XVII

Anne plugged her mobile phone into the charger and left it on the bedside night table. She went straight to her desk and turned on her laptop. While the configuration loaded, she took off her shoes, pants, and socks. She preferred to work comfortably, and avoid the clothing pressure on her skin.

She began typing at a dizzying speed. The information was so recent that she didn't need to listen to the recording. That would have been a slower and more tedious process. Not all recorded material is suitable for writing a report, as she usually discarded more than half of it. And listening to everything was a waste of time, time she didn't have if she wanted to write *a good shit* to please Ben.

She wrote a suggestion for the headline: "Possible Ambitious Young Man Behind Murders of Two Widows in Sylvanville." And then continued:

"The police have no reliable information to suggest that it is an ambitious and unscrupulous young man who has killed the two women in the Evergreen neighbourhood, but if it is, how many more victims could there be in other states?"

"This is going to hurt, Mayor Thorne." And she continued typing for the editorial:

"A a voluntary collaborator with this reporter, has opened a new line of investigation based on observations by the street's residents. He believes that these are well-organized murders in an attempt to rob the women off or force them to change their will in their favour..."

"You wanted something made up, Benjamin Pierce? I hope you like it, and if not, add some salt and swallow it," she said to the screen.

When she finished writing, it was almost three in the afternoon. She called the newsroom to give some instructions.

"Write it in big, red letters. Don't skimp on the size," she explained to the designer. "Ask for an image of Evergreen Street. Maybe there's something in the archives from the moment the victims were found... You know, yellow tape around the lampposts, blue lights spinning... Perfect! Call me if you need any further information. Hugs."

She sat on the bed and fell back onto the mattress. She took a deep breath and exhaled slowly. She thought about taking a relaxing bath. She had brought some toys, and when she was about to take them out of the suitcase, the screen's brightness caught her attention. There was a new message from the person.

She read it and got scared and forwarded it to Mike immediately. The phone rang within a few seconds.

"Well done, Anne. I think we've killed a pawn. Or a bishop. We'll see. The important thing is to keep pressuring until the king falls. Are you feeling better?"

"I think so. At least I didn't have a panic attack when this message arrived. I think I'm getting used to being blackmailed."

"No, no, no. You're getting used to a guy like me becoming your bodyguard in Sylvanville."

"You're right, Mike. I think if you weren't here, I would have taken the interstate days ago, stepped on the accelerator and would have time-travelled like the DeLorean in *Back to the Future*. I would have left my town hundreds of kilometres away..."

"It's our city, Anne. Ours, and no one is going to take it away from us. I'll be there in fifteen minutes. We'll plan the next move on the board and celebrate the day with good wine." Michael interrupted her and made the proposal.

"I've heard there's a great play at the Starlight Theatre. A musical, I think I read on the town hall's Facebook page."

"Great. I'll go to the website and buy the tickets before they sell out. You might run into your mayor, Mr. Edwin Thorne."

"That wouldn't be bad. I'd like to see his face today and tomorrow, after the Daily Beacon hits the stands, to see the before and after," she laughed.

"Well, well. Does that sound like revenge to me?"

"No. It's about venting. These have been the worst eight days of my life in Sylvanville. Or at least, I don't remember feeling this way before."

"I understand you perfectly. I have good news. I also sat down in front of the computer and managed to advance ten thousand words. This case opens up the hope of tying together some ideas that I had conceived. The fact that the murdered women are widows also works in my favour."

"And what if in the end the entire hypothesis has nothing to do with reality?" she expressed with fear.

"And who told you that I write reality? Fiction, Anne. The best thing in the world is fiction."

"A foolish conceited man," she replied in a mocking tone.

"Very well. Get dolled up and gorgeous. Let's go to the theatre after the matter."

"Perfect. I think it will do us good. I'll be waiting for you."

In fifteen minutes, she would have time for a bath and to relax before Michael arrived, so she continued with the plan and brought an electric water prove dildo into the bathtub.

Before Michael touched the intercom, Anne was dressed, except for some accessories and makeup. It took her a little while to decide because she wasn't sure about the dress code for that play and venue. She placed a long, flared dark pantsuit in each corner of the bed, like a combat ring, which she knew looked very elegant on her. If she paired it with low-heeled shoes, it could be one of the options.

And in the other corner of the ring, there was a long burgundy dress, also elegant and a bit more sophisticated, covering the neck and leaving the shoulders and a suggestive open line on the back sensually exposed.

When she tried both on and combined them with accessories —small earrings and a delicate necklace she had recently bought— she decided on the first one. Her makeup could be subtle, and she planned to put her hair up in a casual ponytail.

"Wow, Anne, how elegant! Now I'm really going to look like a fool next to you," Michael said.

"Don't overdo it. The suit looks good on you, and I love that daring tie for a guy your age," she replied, pinching his cheeks. "And besides, being a fool is irreparable."

"Thank you, thank you. It's a compliment to remind me of my age and qualities."

"We're the same age. Don't worry. Plus, you know women age worse than men."

"Except for you. You haven't changed since your twenties until now."

"Fool! Come on, let's solve the message."

"There's not much to solve. It's asking us to leave the money next to the guard's booth before crossing the wooden bridge."

"What if someone comes and takes it?"

"I'll be right there. I won't leave. I'll bring my bike and two very different types of clothing. I've thought of everything. Underneath my clothes, I'll be ready with the outfit. I have a reversible backpack. I'll store my pants, shirt, and coat and transform into a casual cyclist. With a helmet and a scarf to keep me warm, they won't be able to know who I am."

"Mr. Whitmore, I don't know why you haven't written another book. You have an imagination that should be cherished, as my grandmother used to say."

"I know. It's one of your favourite phrases. So, to the theatre?", he hurried her.

"Straight ahead, sir!"

"Tomorrow we will unmask the blackmailer," said Michael in a subdued voice as they left the apartment.

Anne crossed her fingers.

XVIII

Another stroke of luck for Oliver Silverman. The next morning, he run into the postman as he was heading to the bookstall. It was not a coincidence. Silverman saw him when he stopped his motorbike in front of Hilda's house and took advantage of the fact that he was sorting through the mailbag, and he crossed the road and made it look like a chance encounter, and greeted him:

"Any letter for my friend Hilda? He asked and then explained: "she is not at home right now."

"It's for this address, but for someone named Diego Garcia," replied the mailman.

"That's him! The young man she rented a bedroom to. He's just gone to work."

"It's a shame. I have to come back later because I need a signature," said the postman.

Silverman offered to sign the receipt and deliver it in person, taking advantage of his trust with that postman. He waited for the postman to leave and had a quick look at the letter, then he slipped it into the neighbour's mailbox and hurried home.

Now he had the name of one of them. The return address revealed the information he needed.

He hurried back to the room and jotted down in his notebook before forgetting: "The letter is from a programming and internet services company."

He had a name, a profession, a profile, and completed the notebook: "Diego, computer engineer, Youline Communications, hardworking employee (when he's not glued to his chair, he dedicates himself to household chores), breakfasts between eight and eight-thirty, rests at eleven..."

He was happy to gather information and was looking forward to give it to Miss Harrington and Mr. Whitmore. Spending time with them had opened a door to the world for him.

"Don't you agree, Adeline? They're wonderful people, aren't they?"

Anne woke up before Michael. After finishing the theatre play, they decided to have one last drink at his apartment. One last drink that didn't end until the early hours of the morning.

She didn't remember what happened after that. When she woke up, Mike was sound asleep and completely naked. She, on the other hand, was wearing her pyjamas.

She took advantage of the fact that he was sleeping and silently watched him. At fifty-four, Michael's body had undergone physical changes as part of the normal aging process. He had gained a few pounds and had slightly less muscle mass. When he was young, Michael was an amateur athlete who never wanted to join any university clubs, but he exercised regularly. Now his skin was well-hydrated and the incipient grey hairs gave him an interesting, cultured look.

He was also still good in bed. In that aspect, he remained vital, like he used to be. She caressed his belly and he suddenly woke up.

"What time is it? The money! I have to go to the meeting," he exclaimed.

"Don't worry. Sleep peacefully. It's still early and the appointment is at noon, around two o'clock in the afternoon. Do you remember?"

"Well, no. I don't remember anything. What potion did we have last night?"

"I think it wasn't so much the alcohol but my lack of habit of drinking. And the tiredness from so many emotions," said Anne.

"Well, I feel like I had drunk a swamp."

"You had. I admit it. It happens a lot to fools."

Both laughed. Michael pulled her close and Anne leaned against his chest.

The cold afternoon in Mountain Brook River Park was peaceful and melancholic. Michael walked quickly along the path he had walked with Anne just a few days ago. The leaves fell slowly and had created a blanket of yellowish-brown colours. Surely, the maintenance staff would remove them the following Monday, as Sundays were for rest and there was only a security checkpoint with some municipal employees to deal with any emergencies, especially branches that could break and fall on the citizens who came to the park.

The cloudy and grey sky threatened rain, but the feeling of cold had decreased and some older people sat wrapped in blankets enjoying the sound of the river and the calmness of the place.

He could see the bridge and next to it the booth and he slowed down as he approached. The leaves crunched under the steps of someone behind him. Michael glanced sideways. It was an older person, perhaps a retiree wearing inappropriate sportswear for the age he appeared to be, but he had a good pace, supporting each short stride on hiking poles. He had a hood covering his thinning head from the cold and a scarf to warm his mouth and nose from the cold air.

Michael stopped to pretend to tie his shoelaces and waited for him to pass. "He seems to be in better shape than me," he thought, while waiting for him to continue his morning exercise routine. The man disappeared around the next bend in the path, and left the way clear of witnesses.

When he reached the booth, he hid the bag behind the garbage tank, just as they had agreed. He looked around to make sure no one had seen him. He checked the time and calculated that returning to the car at a fast pace and returning disguised as a cyclist would take him just seven minutes, five if he hurried. He retraced his steps and ran in sections, but the cold air made him cough and stop to catch his breath.

He entered the passenger seat to take off his clothes, and the winter cycling tights began to appear as he undressed. "I look like Superman," he thought and smiled. He opened the trunk and took out the bike.

"Damn!" He had forgotten the windbreaker in the bag with the money. "What a blunder, but it's a short stretch, Michael, don't get upset!" he encouraged himself.

He hurried to pedal and make up for lost time on the way back to the car. He would circle around the bag or hide until the time passed. The municipal cameras were recording. It would be a matter of patience, although he feared the cold for cycling the whole time. When he arrived, he leaned the bike against a tree and rushed to the bag to rescue the coat.

The bag was gone!

XIX

He cursed: "Who the hell...?"

He pulled at his hair in desperation. He spun around quickly to try to identify someone carrying the bag. There weren't many people around. He hadn't taken the path back to the car park, because that person would have stumbled upon it on the trail.

"Can't be far, that son of a bitch!" he yelled furiously. With clenched fists, he spun around, trying to spot him. He had lost control. He returned to the car, started it, and began a chaotic tirade of curses as he pounded the steering wheel with both hands.

His head was spinning and he couldn't focus on the chessboard. Someone had snatched an important chess piece from him. He drove erratically through the town streets. He left the park without a direction and in a few minutes, he was crossing Washington Square, the emblematic spot where tourist bus excursions departed. He left the historic centre behind and headed south along Lincoln Avenue, a wide street flanked by many shops, restaurants, and commercial establishments, and turned onto the quiet Maplewood, the most pampered residential area of the town, where affluent families lived in large single-family homes of varying sizes and similar styles, with gardens in the front and green backyards, many of which had designer swimming pools. The wide, tree-lined streets were always clean, and residents lived in a peaceful atmosphere, frequently patrolled by local police.

Maplewood ended at a small hill crowned by a lookout. Michael's Chevrolet Spark ascended more calmly and parked near the viewpoint. He got out of the car and walked the short distance to the hill with excellent views of the valley and the town. He took a deep breath of fresh evening air to try to relax.

This place was a mandatory stop for tourists. The road signs said Hillside Lookout, although during his college years, the students changed the name to Crystal Hill Lookout due to the number of bottles they left behind after weekend parties. The students felt safer because if the police drove up the road, they could spot them coming in advance and descend on a dirt path back to town.

From the lookout, the town stretched out majestically before the eyes of locals and visitors, and the views changed with the four seasons of the year. Now it was the turn of the winter landscape.

Some old buildings contrasted with the modern ones that proudly rose on the outskirts of the city, the areas of expansion from the old historic centre. The river snaked through its course, almost unchanged for generations, dividing Sylvanville from the agricultural areas on the other side of the park where Anne had just lost her money.

The farmland, covered by a thin blanket of snow, created an impressive contrast with the intense green of spring and summer.

Farther away, locals and tourists could enjoy the outline of the small Saint Mary's Church of the Fields, which seemed to be suspended in the air, evoking the arrival of the first settlers who began to cultivate the land and sowed the seeds of the current Sylvanville.

He continued to breathe slowly and deeply and tried to think which piece of the chess game he would move. It was his turn. A feeling of helplessness overwhelmed him.

"Checkmate?" he asked himself. He couldn't get out of the deadlock and felt he was losing the game due to rashness, immaturity, or foolishness, as Anne had always told him; and for rushing, and for so many mistakes...

He returned to the car when the cold air became uncomfortable and before putting the key in the ignition, he had an idea: he would report the theft of the bag to the police.

He started the car and roamed stress-free and went back over his steps, driving the same roads that led to the historic town centre that housed the town hall and police facilities.

He parked in the underground car park under Washington Square and went to the reporting office:

"Good afternoon," he said calmly. "I would like to report the theft of a bag with personal belongings in the forest park."

XX

Anne woke up to a call from the Daily Beacon. It was Megan Hayes, Benjamin's assistant, the editor-in-chief.

"Hi, Anne. I hope I didn't wake you up," said Megan.

"Don't worry, Meg. I was already awake," Anne lied. "How is the boss doing today?" she asked with some concern. Her article was already out.

"He's thrilled! It seems like you've hit a nerve with the mayor of your city. He just called the newsroom and spent a good while complaining about your article," Megan said.

"Good to hear. Then I hit the nail on the head, "Anne smiled.

"And loud and clear! Let me put you through to Mr. Pierce. He asked me to find you."

"Okay, Meg. Take care. See you soon."

"Same to you, darling. We miss you in the newsroom."

The line waited with a calm jazz piece that didn't loop. It was Anne's idea, as she found it reassuring in case the caller had to wait for a long time. Every fifteen seconds, a gentle female voice interrupted the music and announced that the call would be answered shortly.

Anne imagined that the boss was answering endless calls from different entities, organizations, groups, companies, and town halls that usually contacted the newspaper to congratulate or to threaten them and announce lawsuits of all kinds.

That's freedom of the press. The truth can be a spur for a business and a disaster for a politician, as was the case. Maintaining a certain number of sales and interest is an important part of the company's policy. The number of readers increased the price that advertisers had to pay for placing their ads in prominent places in the newspaper.

"Anne! Wonderful job. You did a good job," Benjamin Pierce said in a commendable tone, very different from the threatening chat of the day before. That's how the boss was.

"Thanks, Ben. I guess I'll need a bodyguard if I want to enter the town hall today," Anne joked.

"If you get stabbed in the back, it means you're on the right track. This group of incompetents has been unable to move the matter in a way that provokes the citizens' interest in the murders and helps to solve it," Benjamin said with sarcasm and some irritation.

"You're right. A scared witness could pull the thread if they see that the authorities and law enforcement back them up," she agreed.

"Well, baby. Keep it up. I spoke with Mayor Thorne. It was a 'thorny' conversation," he laughed loudly at his own joke, "he showed off his 'sharp-nosed' family name. I wouldn't be surprised if he calls you right now."

"I hope so. I think I can convince him to work together. See you later, boss."

"Take care. A hug."

Anne hadn't even finished her conversation with Benjamin Pierce when her phone rang again. She looked at the screen and the caller ID indicated it was the official phone of the Sylvanville Town Hall. Anne wanted to freshen up, have a coffee, and get dressed to face the day. She let it ring and trusted the formal message of the answering machine: "Hello, this is Anne Harrington. I am unable to take your call at the moment. Please leave me a phone number and I will get back to you as soon as possible. Thank you."

She looked at the time. She was worried that Michael hadn't called or sent a message since the previous day. She feared the worst: that no one had gone to pick up the bag and they were still at the same starting point: having to deal with a threat from something that had happened in the past that could shake and topple the foundations of the present... and the future.

She was uneasy and decided not to call him right away, but she needed to prepare and be available for the meeting with Mayor Thorne. She urgently needed a long coffee to recharge her batteries.

At least she was pleased with the work and the praising conversation with her boss. That gave her some leeway in the professional world to be able to focus on getting to the bottom of personal issues.

While her friend showered and dealt with guilt and daily tasks, Michael waited on the road. He parked on the sidewalk in front of the apartments where Anne lived. He hadn't taken off his seat belt. He was staring ahead through the windshield without noticing the traffic and urban life that passed as usual.

He had been sitting like this for a while with the desire to go up and wake her up with breakfast in bed, but he had a knot in his stomach that prevented him from acting. Finally, he took out the copy of the police report from the glove compartment and read it again. He skipped the header that contained the personal data of the report, the date, the place, and a title:

"He declares that a black polyester bag without any identifying label has been stolen, containing personal items: a wristwatch valued at $500, a wallet with cash estimated at around $300, bank cards, and warm clothing. According to the victim, he had gone to the park to ride his bike and had placed the bag on the lid of the trash can next to the bridge booth. When he realized his mistake and returned, it was gone."

"Mr. Whitmore, there are surveillance cameras in the park and throughout the town. With a court order, we will begin investigating immediately. Be certain that the person who took that bag will be identified, punished, and you will be able to recover your belongings," said the officer who attended Michael. The officer claimed it could be someone from the town. With the extreme winter they were experiencing, he didn't believe that criminals from other places were lurking in Sylvanville.

After reading it, he calmed down. He was sure that movement of the chess piece on the board was the best option (he didn't have many more). If the thief made the money disappear, at least the police could give him a name and last name. Then he would personally take care of settling accounts, he thought. Half a million dollars isn't spent overnight. He knew the ostentatious idiosyncrasies of the citizens: someone would buy a latest model car or invest in luxurious house renovations soon or late.

He only had one detail left that had kept him in the car with his seat belt fastened: what would he say to Anne?

He was unable to find an answer so, he decided to leave and surrender to his creative mind as soon as he got to the apartment...

"Hi, Mike!" she exclaimed when she opened the door. She was wrapped in a bath towel, drying her hair. "I'm glad to see you. I was really worried when I didn't hear from you. What happened with the bag?"

"I decided to change the strategy on the fly," he made up.

"In what way?" she asked as she put in an earring.

"Well, I thought that police intervention could resolve the issue. I don't know... I thought maybe he's a dangerous guy and he could keep blackmailing us and making us lose all our savings."

"Okay. And what happened?"

"I let him take the bag."

"You let him take half a million dollars!?" Anne turned red. "But how are you going to get that money back?"

"Very easy. I reported the robbery to the police. There are cameras all over the park and the town. This person can be tracked anywhere, and they assured me that it would be very easy to locate the person, report them, and bring them to justice."

"Of course. And then he'll tell the judge that we were responsible for an accident."

"No. He won't say anything. I talked to William Archer, my lawyer friend. He says that everything is past the statute of limitations, that without evidence (and after three decades) there's no case and no possibility at all," he lied.

"And have you confessed that a person died because of our fault?"

"It was an accident, Anne! It was involuntary. We weren't murderers. Archer gave me all the guarantees. There's no case. No witnesses. No evidence," Michael counted on his fingers. "Don't you think the person blackmailing us would have already reported it? This is just a strategy to make easy money. Trust me."

"Why didn't you find out before taking half a million dollars for a walk in the park?"

"You're right," he apologised and after a pause he took to continue the story: "I was a fool and I let myself be driven by fear and the need to take care of you. Your career. I beg you to forgive me and let me recover everything. I want to definitively close the door on that dark room that hasn't let us live. Lock the ghost inside tightly and enjoy the life we have left."

Anne felt compassion. She knew that Michael Whitmore, her most loyal friend from youth, would do anything for her. He always did. Young Mike had the spirit of a guardian angel and defended her in any circumstance and against anyone, even when she knew she was wrong. Michael didn't care, he always stood up for her.

They hugged.

"What are you going to do today?" Michael asked.

"I think I'll have to go to the town hall soon. Yesterday we opened Pandora's box."

"Has Mr. Thorne called you?"

"I haven't spoken to him yet, but Mr. Thorne has a 'thorn' in his chest and I think he'll try to remove it by inviting me to participate in the investigation of the cases," she explained, pointing to her heart.

"Has he offered it to you?"

"Not yet, but he will soon. Can you take me to the town hall?"

XXI

Oliver Silverman was awakened in the early morning by the sirens and police car lights that illuminated the room, making it to look like a blue-strobe-lighted night club. He peeked through the "rear window", grabbed his binoculars, and observed the scene at his neighbour's house. He jotted down in his notebook, "Three police cars parked at Hilda's house. The nephew opens the door. Diego comes downstairs. 'Hilda, dead, river...'"

He went to bed when the street quieted down and tuned in to the local channel. The news was headlining, and the regular programming had been interrupted to broadcast from the scene of the discovery. The reporter appeared in front of a shrub near the river and a rarely travelled path that led to that side of the bank. He raised the volume with the remote control and listened attentively:

"A third victim has been found on the shore of Mountain Brook River. The police have identified her as Watson's widow, Hilda Watson, an eighty-year-old resident of Evergreen. She appears to have suffered a head injury, which may have been the cause of death.

Currently, there is no further information or apparent motivation that the investigators have found..."

Silverman took his notepad and made some notes: "Hilda found dead in the river: murdered?" He added a question mark, awaiting more information that could help him solve the mystery. He immediately thought of his beloved writer and journalist.

"Adeline! We're getting closer to the end, darling. I think we'll have another visitor today. I know you're happy about it... They're so friendly!"

Anne Harrington's phone rang on her way to the town hall. The voice of a young lady identifying herself as a clerk from the mayor's office informed her that Mr. Edwin Thorne would like to see her to assist in the investigation of the Sylvanville murders.

"Alright. I'm on my way. It'll take..." She glanced at Michael, who raised his right hand with open fingers. "...about five minutes. Or ten, I don't think it'll be longer."

She said goodbye and looked at Michael with a wide smile.

"You're a witch, Miss Harrington. You can see the future."

"It's not that. They tried to contact me an hour ago. I know how politicians work. Government offices are full of intrigues and backstabbing. I've learned to push the right buttons to make them eat out of my hand."

"When threats with the press come into play, they turn into docile little creatures. Believe me."

"Not only do I believe you. I think the same as you. In general, citizens know that power hooks them more than true love for the community. If the state or the country flourishes, they succeed, I mean, their ego and personal economy. Perhaps that's the reason for seeking development and well-being. That's why I believe you do a necessary job. That way, at least, we can keep them in check and teach them a lesson when they go too far."

Both of them laughed.

"We do a job," Anne corrected him. "I'm not the only reporter in the country."

"For me, you are."

Michael accompanied her to the town hall. He mentioned that while she spoke with the mayor, he would go back to the police to look for any updates regarding the purse investigation.

"Miss Harrington! It is a honour and a pleasure to have you back in this house, which is yours," he flattered her excessively. Anne hoped it would be so. "Would you like anything?"

"Thank you very much, Mayor. I just had a coffee, and it didn't sit well with my stomach."

"I'm really sorry... Ahem!... I spoke with the editor-in-chief of the Daily Beacon just a couple of hours ago. He's a pleasant man, to be honest."

Anne would not have described Benjamin Pierce with that particular quality, but she was not a politician in need of appearances either.

"I'm glad that our report has generated interest. Do you think the police will now have a lead to follow?" she said ironically.

"In fact, we have a suspect and... another body."

"Another body? Do you mind if I record the conversation?" Anne always preferred the complete content, the raw material, to shape it later as necessary.

"I kindly request this information not be recorded. But you can take whatever notes you deem appropriate."

Anne looked at him with disappointment. She had imagined he would reject the proposal. But, after all, it was less painful than a stab in the back.

"Of course, certainly," she replied amiably, rummaging in her bag and pulling out a notepad and a pen. "So, who is it?"

"It's the widow of Watson, Hilda Watson. She resided on Evergreen Lane."

Anne's heart skipped a beat. Oliver Silverman had feared something like this had happened to his neighbour for weeks. No one had reported her disappearance, and she remembered the young man who had forcefully entered the house. But she kept her sources to herself.

"And what do we know about it?" she probed the mayor.

"Well, she was found on the riverbank, about two miles past the bridge on the right side. According to the investigators, she died there, meaning someone must have taken her alive and then struck her in the head.

There are no signs of a struggle at Mrs. Watson's house. If we add that to the location of the discovery, the investigators believe the suspect is someone from this city who knows the trail and had a good relationship with Hilda. Perhaps a close relative."

"And when did the death occur?"

"They are still working on the examination. But due to the state of decomposition, the body has been there for many days."

"So, she died from a blow to the head. Nothing else? Just one blow?" Anne asked, barely finishing writing the last sentence.

"The investigators confirm that it was a single blow with a blunt and heavy object, perhaps a hammer. As I told you, they are conducting the autopsy today."

"What motivated the attack?"

"It's unknown," Thorne insisted. "They are currently questioning the detainee, who claims to have no connection to the victim. He simply occupied the house after noticing it was vacant. The neglected garden, old newspapers, and so on. He doesn't appear to be the killer, at least not at first glance."

"Are you sure that's all the information you have, Mayor?" she asked incisively, placing the notepad on the mayor's desk.

"Well... But I need this information to remain confidential. I kindly request that you guard it diligently until it can be revealed."

Anne raised her left hand and placed her right hand on the notepad, as if it were a bible, and swore on her honour that she would not disclose the information, but that she would have the exclusive story if necessary.

"I trust you, Miss Harrington. I know you care about Sylvanville and its inhabitants... The killer tried to clean up the blood from the scene," the mayor revealed, lowering his voice.

"But if it had seeped into the ground, the rain would have made it disappear," Anne commented, surprised. "What do the investigators think?"

"They're unsure if the killer attempted to remove the blood, even if it was mixed with the soil. Perhaps some satanic ritual? You know how many criminal lunatics roam this planet we inhabit."

"You're absolutely right, Mayor. I appreciate the information, which I will handle discreetly. And, as you said, in favour of our beloved community."

"I wanted to mention... uh! In relation to your excellent reports," the mayor hesitated. "May I ask you a favour?"

"Yes, of course. That's what the Daily Beacon is for, to benefit the citizens and the administrations," she responded sarcastically once again. She wanted to highlight that he hadn't been sincere during the previous visit and likely alerted the police chief not to provide her with information.

"We would like your reports to have our collaboration. The city council and the police are at your disposal. It will be my personal commitment to your important outlet. But we would also like you to help us... let's say... I don't know if 'filtering' is the right word."

"You don't mean 'censor,' do you?" Thorne turned red.

"No, no, no. Not at all! I mean a commitment to publish information that doesn't hinder the investigation and highlights the values of our officers and the work of this city council."

"That sounds like a fair deal, Mayor Thorne. I am willing to 'filter' and enhance the city, and you are willing not to 'skimp' on providing information," she said, feeling victorious. Thorne seemed smaller in that pompous chair now.

"How glad I am! Rest assured, I will keep you informed, and you know, consider the city council your home as well."

"One last request, Mr. Thorne. Could I inquire about an accident that happened a long time ago?" Anne took the opportunity to open doors.

"Of course. I will call the police chief immediately to arrange the best way for you to access the file," the mayor agreed helpfully.

"Thank you very much. Very kind of you. We'll stay in touch."

"It will be a pleasure." Thorne bid her farewell with a handshake and a smile that nearly dislocated his jaw.

Anne walked out triumphantly and descended the stairs swiftly. Michael told her he had news and that they would meet in the lobby of the town hall to have lunch together. "Sylvan's Corner?" she asked, and he responded with the "ok" emoji.

"How did everything go?" Michael asked her, looking serious.

"Perfectly! Just as planned."

Anne was happy, which reassured Michael. However, he had just figured out who had stolen the bag, and the anguish tightened his chest.

"Do you mind if I stop by the police chief's office before we go to Sylvan's? It'll only take five minutes," Anne asked him.

"Of course. Sure. I'll be right there," Michael pointed to the wooden benches near the information booth at the entrance of the building.

"Thanks, Mike. I'll be quick. I'm hungry and thirsty now, but not for revenge," she smiled.

Michael forced a smile and walked with his head down. He sat down, leaned back, placed his elbows on his thighs, and rested his head in his hands, like a punished child at school. Unlike Anne, the release of the police video had taken away his appetite. He remained lost in thought, contemplating his next move on the chessboard.

"Here are the images from the different park cameras. We've searched for the chronological sequence, from the moment you arrive and leave the bag, to when you return to your car," the officer said as he played various recordings. "And in this sequence, the person who took the bag arrives. We can't identify the face. Pay attention to how the hat covers the head, and the suspect wears a scarf and dark glasses that make facial recognition impossible. Our conclusion is that it's a man, shorter than you, elderly... Based on their walking style, we would say their age is around eighty..."

Michael believed he knew the figure who took the bag. He had no doubt that it was one of his fervent followers: Oliver Silverman.

XXII

The police department was located right next to the town hall building. It also had an imposing appearance. The entrance had double doors with bulletproof glass for small-calibre weapons.

Anne passed through the security checkpoint in the visitor reception area. There was a sign that said "general inquiries," and she approached a uniformed officer who was attending to some citizens.

"Miss Harrington, the chief is waiting for you," the officer pointed to the stairs with the same pen she had been holding since she noticed Anne. Anne thought that Edwin was keeping his commitment, perhaps to demonstrate through his actions that she should also fulfil her promise. That was not a problem for Anne; her word was worth more than the sum of oaths from all the rulers of Sylvanville town and its districts.

She climbed the stairs and immediately saw the sign on the door that read "Anderson Parker, Chief."

"Excuse me, chief," Anne said and entered the office with an air of pretentiousness, as if she were the owner of the police station.

"Miss Harrington," exclaimed Parker, who was waiting for her after the mayor called him directly. "Let me know how we can assist you. We are at your service."

"Well, Mr. Parker, you know that I am collaborating in the investigation of the three widows' murder, but I am here for another inquiry," explained Anne.

"If we can answer your questions, we will do so. The mayor ordered us to provide you with all the information you need, Miss Harrington. We are at your service, ma'am," he repeated.

"About thirty years ago, there was an accident on the park road, I think it was by Forest Road at the crossing with Sylvan Way. It was a winter afternoon, and there was some ice on the road. The vehicle involved in the accident was traveling towards the city with two passengers. Another vehicle hit it as it left the crossing without stopping at the STOP sign."

"Yes, I vaguely recall it being mentioned in the office. However, at that time, I wasn't a police officer yet."

"I see. My intention is to review the case file to complete my report."

"Hold a second, please. I have the person who can assist you," Parker said, picked up the phone and dialled a number. "John, reporter Anne Harrington from the Daily Beacon will be coming down in a second to inquire about an old case file. She will brief you... Thank you." He hung up the phone and said to Anne: "ask for Officer Martin and request her to accompany you to the archives. I'll be here just in case you need further assistance."

"Thank you very much, Chief Parker. I'm sure the Daily Beacon will appreciate your confidence in me," she said as she shook his hand in farewell.

Officer Martin accompanied Anne to the lift door. She pressed the call button.

"Miss Harrington, press the 'archives' button, and you'll go directly to the department," she pointed from outside the elevator as the doors closed.

"Thank you very much, Officer. I'll do that," Anne replied with a smile.

The local police archive in Sylvanville was a roomy area with perfectly aligned shelves. It was located in the basement, and Anne felt a slight sense of suffocation, although they had tried to improve the atmosphere by adding bright lighting and a suitable temperature to make it somewhat welcoming. Compared to the space she enjoyed at the Daily Beacon's editorial office, it felt like a dungeon to her. The advantage was the architect's idea of installing a lift to connect the agents' workspace on the upper floor with the filing area. It was very convenient.

Without crossing the protective gate which separated the small reception area from the secure zone where millions of documents on the town's criminal history were stored, Anne saw several sections marked with signs dedicated to different types of crimes: reports, ongoing investigations, closed cases, pending cases, arrest records, officers' personal files, among others.

Anne filled out the entry registration form, and the officer granted her access and led her to the end of a row.

The evidence boxes changed colour as they walked down the hallway, as if the oldest ones were at the very end. And that turned out to be true.

The officer reached out and took a labelled box. Anne could only see a year printed on the label, 1993.

The officer carried the box back to the entrance and placed it on a large table. He broke the seal, made some notes on the file registration form, and pulled out a report. Anne clearly understood the importance they attached to security and privacy protocols after the access controls and the treatment the file had received. The Sylvanville police had a well-organized archive, which gave her confidence that she would find the information about her past secret.

Anne Harrington felt the heat rising up her neck as the moment approached to read the documents contained in that navy blue file. She was about to confront the worst scene she had ever experienced in her life, and her hands began to tremble.

She opened the folder. The first pages provided general information about the location, date, and briefly summarized the affected vehicle and victims.

Then she read carefully. Her mouth dropped open, and she felt breathless. She sat down. She nearly lost consciousness when she discovered the name of the person who had died in the accident.

XXIII

She was about to cry: "Adeline Silverman?!", but she choked back a scream to avoid drawing the attention of the officer in charge of the archive, who was engrossed in watching a football match on his mobile phone. The commentator's voice he was listening to through his headphones helped mask her exclamation.

She had to sit down and take a deep breath. The muscles in her arm went limp, and the document slipped off the table. The accident was an unsolved case. They never found the person responsible for causing the collision with the Silvermans' vehicle, which resulted in the instant death of Adeline Silverman, a forty-five-year-old woman, and caused severe burns to her husband, Oliver Silverman, who was forty-eight years old.

Her heart pounded heavily, and she couldn't hold back the urge to cry. When she saw the faces of the victims on the photographs, Anne Harrington felt dirty, and the sense of guilt she had tried to control for so many years immediately surfaced.

She tried to stifle her sobs to avoid attracting attention from the officer. She wiped away her tears and asked if she could use the restroom because she was feeling unwell.

"Of course," he replied, removing the earpiece from his left ear. "Just at the end of the table, there's a hallway to the right. It's the first door," he pointed, barely taking his eyes off the small phone screen.

Anne hurried with long strides despite her trembling legs. She held back the nausea until she reached the first stall in the toilet. She knelt down, and her stomach expelled thirty years of guilt. She sat on the floor, gasping for air from the strain on her muscles, and leaned her back against the tiled wall. She took deep breaths as many times as necessary to control the racing palpitations, fatigue, and dizziness that prevented her from moving.

She was paralyzed, and questions flooded her mind like an avalanche of uncertainties about her future from that moment on.

She was overwhelmed by the need to unburden herself and share the weight with someone who could help, and she remembered that Mike, her guardian angel, was waiting for her in the town hall lobby. Now she would have to try to deal with the intense emotions, and she thought about all the relaxation strategies and techniques that her therapist had advised her.

After a few minutes, she struggled to get up. She saw her reflection in the bathroom mirror. The tears had diluted her makeup and distorted her features. Suddenly, she saw herself as a selfish villain, capable of leaving Oliver Silverman, the charming old man who had welcomed her into his home with such kindness, on the road, and not seeking help from emergency services that might have saved his wife's life, the one he kept alive, mentioning her in conversations. She imagined the deep loneliness Oliver must have endured for so many decades, longing for Adeline.

And she had a responsibility in that tragedy. She turned on the water and repeatedly splashed her face, sobbing, removing all the makeup to erase the face of the despicable person she had just seen in front of her. Her 1993 self, a reckless and careless young woman who got into a car with friends who had been drinking alcohol, acting rashly and without thinking, shouting challenges to the citizens of Sylvanville from the railing of Crystal Hill Lookout, and she incessantly asked herself "why?" She couldn't put herself in the shoes of that moment and understand herself.

Gradually, she began to calm down. After another five minutes, she managed to catch her breath and decided to return to the table, retrieve her purse, and apply makeup again.

The file was still open on the table, and several photographs, which had probably been taken while she rushed to the bathroom, displayed the aftermath of the accident involving the wrecked vehicle, a red 1990 Ford Mustang.

She struggled to apply makeup as her hands still trembled, but for her, it was more important to leave the archive, which had suddenly turned into a catacomb where the ghosts of the past, Adeline and Oliver Silverman, lay.

Anne mumbled words of gratitude to the archive custodian. Impatiently, she pressed the elevator button several times. She left the police building and walked briskly.

"Michael!" she managed to say when she met her friend. "We killed Oliver Silverman's wife!"

XXIV

Oliver Silverman jotted down in his notepad the conclusions that the police explained on television. The autopsy was conducted quickly, confirming that the cause of death was a blow to the head, resulting in a fracture of the occipital bone.

That day, he bought a copy of the local newspaper, as the discovery was given much prominence on the front page.

According to the initial information, the body was found by cyclists who were riding along the trail near the riverbank. It had been hidden in the undergrowth for several days, hence why it had gone unnoticed, but the smell alerted the athletes, who initially thought it was some wild animal.

For Silverman, everything was unfolding as he had imagined. That young man could be the culprit. If called to testify, he would have enough information to create a profile. For example, he emphasized the word "inheritance" in his notes and added a question mark. Could that be the motive he would present to the police?

Another factor working against the neighbour's luck was that she lived alone, and rarely did any family members visit the house. She had no children, only two nieces, daughters of her late older sister. They lived far away and only visited on special occasions, not always.

He reviewed his notebook's notes and rubbed off the question mark from the sentence, "Will they find the body someday?" which he had written after that "nephew" arrived at the house. It had already happened.

"The nephew is the key," he insisted, underlining the phrase and tapping the tip of his pen. Soon, he would resolve his concerns.

Anne had no appetite to eat at Sylvan's, and neither did Michael. They drove back to Anne's apartment in silence.

As a writer, Michael tried to formulate a mental outline: a name, Oliver Silverman, crossed their path, they met at Sylvan's Corner, was it by chance? He is the husband of the victim from the accident they caused in 1993.

On the chessboard, there were fewer and fewer pieces, yet despite that, the game seemed to be reaching its end, and they were at a standstill.

For Michael, Silverman was the king. For Anne, he was the collateral victim of an involuntary manslaughter. As the officer guarding the door informed her, homicide cases never expire. They are classified as "unsolved," and a specialized unit takes care of dusting off leads and analysing events from different points of view, using modern scientific resources that advance each year.

Any investigator, at any time, could walk down the same hallway of the police archive she had walked through and retrieve the contents of the box, apply modern techniques, and arrive at different conclusions.

It would be the end of her career. She would probably be sentenced to years in prison and would have to live with real killers and girls who ended up in jail for being troublesome, not for being journalists or writers for a major national media paper. She would be the only woman who didn't fit in there. Just the thought of it made her feel claustrophobic.

She had already done reports on women's prisons and had watched the series *Orange Is the New Black* with interest. She imagined herself in that scenario, with aggressive, uncouth people, and couldn't hold back the urge to cry.

Michael reached out and placed his hand on her thigh to try to calm her, but he couldn't succeed.

Michael thought he had a pending conversation with Oliver Silverman. He needed to clarify certain financial matters. How had he managed to send the message, especially that last message? "Damn old man!" he thought angrily.

The money didn't belong to him. He decided that same afternoon he would dust off her 9mm Glock and go to the shooting range to practice. It had been a while since he had used it, and he was out of practice, but he needed to make sure Silverman didn't have an ace up his sleeve.

"You told me that William Archer claimed that the statute of limitations had expired for the homicide after so many decades. Why did you lie to me?" Anne broke the silence between sobs.

"It wasn't exactly that. I tried not to worry you. I said they would need evidence and witnesses from something that happened so long ago."

"Silverman can be a witness. What if he identifies us!? We witnessed the accident, or rather, we crashed into his car. You spoke to him, he begged us to call an ambulance, he pleaded for his wife's life..." Anne broke down crying and between sobs added: "We left, Mike! We left the scene, and she died. Can you estimate the damage we caused?"

Anne never got over the recurring image of the accident. They were a couple, more or less young from the current perspective. Today, she was older than Adeline Silverman was at the time of the accident. They cut short the life and health of a couple, more or less young too.

Suddenly, she understood why Oliver used the wheelchair as Adeline recommended, or why he served the table and justified it by saying his wife would eat later, why he shouted as if she were in the adjacent room. Poor Oliver Silverman hadn't overcome the blow either and had tried to live a life with a fictional character that he kept alive. He had taken the worst part.

"Anne, look at me! We need to unlock ourselves and think rationally," Michael held her wrists.

"Do you think Oliver is the person from the messages?" she asked, her cheeks soaked with tears.

"I'm convinced he is. Let's recap. When he met us at Sylvan's Corner..., I don't think that meeting was a coincidence."

"Are you suggesting he orchestrated the encounter... and took my phone to see the number? I don't usually lock the screen with a security code," she expressed with concern.

"It's the most likely scenario," Michael affirmed.

"But we're talking about an eighty-year-old person who takes notes in a notebook because he doesn't like or understand technology," she supposed.

"Those could be appearances, just like the wheelchair, just like talking to Adeline. You should have seen how agile he was on the park trail. Oliver Silverman is hiding something from us. He probably planned revenge."

Anne reflected for a moment and calmly said: "and we're public figures. It's easy to track us since we started to stand out. I even announced on my social media that I would be back in Sylvanville to work on the report."

"I believe so. Oliver Silverman has spent a lifetime meticulously planning revenge, and upon learning that the reporter, Anne Harrington, would come to investigate the crimes, he took advantage of it to see us."

"How did he know we would be at Sylvan's Corner?", questioned Anne.

"Who didn't go to Sylvan's Corner in 1993?" Michael asked, but he was claiming there was no other answer. "It's likely that after the accident, he would have tracked us down, but he couldn't testify against us. No one had evidence, and we could create a solid alibi with dozens of friends covering for us, saying we went out with the car."

"Of course. And your mother took it to Max's garage the next morning because she urgently needed it for the new job," Anne recalled. Then she fell silent, trying to organize her thoughts, and asked, "What will we do if we go to his house?"

"Recover the money."

"Right. But that doesn't solve the problem. It's merely trading a pawn for a queen. I prefer for him to keep the money, for us to acknowledge our guilt. That would be the best move from my point of view," Anne clarified.

"I think we should take down the king."

"Don't you dare!" Anne shouted angrily.

"It's just a figure of speech."

"I'm not in the mood for jokes, Mike. This is very serious. Silverman knows that we're responsible for Adeline's death," she cried out in desperation once again.

Michael fell silent and pondered. What would a writer do with the character in the end? He had to think about resolving the conflict. If it were fiction, he wouldn't hesitate to eliminate Silverman. With his death and no witnesses, the case would be closed. But he also faced the challenge of how to remove him. It would have to be a natural death caused by age. A gunshot with his Glock? Using a registered weapon was an absurd idea.

Mr. Silverman would invite them for tea or coffee. What if some harmless poisonous substance fell into his cup...? Anne wouldn't have to know.

XXV

Silverman scribbled in his notepad that the police had once again come to Hilda's house. This time, he was the one who called the emergency hotline to report a suspected crime in the neighbour's house, the poor Mrs. Watson, who was found in the river.

"Yes, Mr. Silverman," the 911 operator responded. The news was on everyone's lips in the city. "Tell me what it's about."

"I have been keeping watch on Hilda Watson's house since the incident, and I believe the tenant has murdered a young man who rented another room in the house. I'm afraid he may have also murdered Mrs. Watson herself... I have reviewed my notes, you know?!"

"When did it happen?"

"Right now, miss."

He then sat and waited to see the bedroom dazzled by the blue flashes of the emergency and police teams.

He aimed his camera at the kitchen, which the forensic police in their white coats were examining.

Camera flashes.

"The nephew seemed disturbed and nervous," he wrote when they put him in a patrol car that disappeared down the street with sirens blaring.

Everything was falling into place. He realized that other officers who stayed at the scene were looking at his window from Hilda's sidewalk and assumed they would come to interview him. As soon as they started crossing the street, the old man anticipated it and went downstairs. He knew exactly what they would ask him. And he had the answers: he wouldn't tell them anything, he didn't know more than what he conveyed to the 911 operator. He saw nothing more, and heard nothing at all.

He needed a little more time. He owed Anne Harrington a good story, and he even had some photos he took through the telescope. He wrote the exact time when "the nephew" stabbed the other person, tied him up, and he saw where he hid the bloodied rope in a hidden corner of the garden.

"Are you sure?" insisted one of the officers. "Didn't you see anyone loitering on the street? Last night, you must have heard noises from a fight... shouts?"

Silverman denied it.

"Your neighbours say you spy on them."

"My neighbours probably don't know that I'm an amateur astronomer. I observe the stars and planets every day," he explained calmly.

"Please call us if you remember anything," the police officer requested.

The old man accepted the card they gave him and slowly closed the door. He went back up to his apartment and waited for the day to arrive.

"Mr. Whitmore, Oliver on the line. How are you?"

The call disturbed Michael. He wasn't expecting any moves on the chessboard at that early hour. He and Anne had gone to bed very late, trying to shape the encounter with Oliver Silverman. The call surprised him because the opponent had beaten him to it.

"Oliver? Has something happened?"

"Yes. I have good news for Miss Harrington's newspaper. I even have excellent photographs," Silverman said excitedly.

"Fantastic, great! I'll tell her as soon as I get in touch with her. Is that okay?"

"Of course. Adeline and I will gladly wait. You can come whenever you like, you know."

Michael Whitmore got out of bed, irritated. That old man had stolen half a million dollars from him and was the number one threat to his future. Not to mention Anne. She was undoubtedly innocent.

"Who were you talking to?" Anne asked as she opened her eyes.

"You won't believe it... With Oliver Silverman."

The sun began to illuminate the skies in the east, tinting the clouds with shades of pink, orange, and gold. As it ascended, the rays of light illuminated the building and spread into Anne's room.

Shops and stores began to open their doors as the roads filled with traffic. Such was the vibrant awakening of the town as it greeted the sunny day.

In the Evergreen area, birds started singing, and neighbours took advantage of the sunny day to go for walks and exercise in the pleasant morning. Oliver Silverman waited patiently, sitting in the desk chair and observing the road through his unique window.

"How are we going to go back to Silverman's house? I would be too embarrassed after discovering that I am partly to blame for his tragic life. I'd rather let him keep the money, Mike. Honestly, I don't care. I think it's terribly unfair that he had to live so many years with that heart-breaking sorrow, locked within himself, without friends, without healthcare..." She paused to swallow a lump. "It moves me that he talks to his wife every day. Perhaps her ghost has kept him alive for so long."

"Hold on, Anne! I don't think he's trying to seek revenge on us. If he found out about our involvement at some point, why would he do something like this now? I think we should meet, ask for and give explanations, bury the ghosts of the past, and help him heal the wound. But he has to return the money to us. We'll figure out a way to compensate somehow."

Anne didn't respond. Michael knew she was pondering his words. He knew her well, and she would likely accept the proposal.

However, he had another move in the game that Anne was unaware of. The intentions were quite different. He wanted to recover the money at all costs and silence Oliver forever. End it with a swift checkmate. He needed just one move to emerge victorious. Now he had to figure out how to do it without Anne noticing.

He would lose her forever.

XXVI

Oliver jumped startled from his seat. He couldn't believe what he was seeing. The "nephew" had returned to Hilda's house. He hadn't suspected that something like this could happen. Perhaps it would have been impossible for the police to find incriminating evidence in the house. The squatter had arrived to Hilda's home long after her disappearance and they might have found out that the guy had a convincing alibi. He had probably been released on bail and ordered to stay in the city.

He seemed restless, and before entering, he looked both ways down the street, fearing being watched. He knew the police would be closely monitoring his movements, and of course, they would probably have asked him not to leave the town, just in case they needed him to answer more questions.

The clock hadn't yet struck noon when the intercom rang. Mr. Whitmore and Miss Harrington had just arrived. Oliver waited behind the door to open it as they reached the landing of his floor.

"Good and wonderful day, dear friends. Please come in," he said.

"Oliver, let's skip the formalities. You know why we're here, right?" Michael went straight to the point.

Silverman looked at him with a puzzled expression. Anne remained motionless, her head bowed and her eyes fixed on the ground, consumed by guilt. The situation was so unpleasant that she felt like running away and never coming back. She couldn't face Oliver Silverman's gaze, and she couldn't swallow the knot tightening her throat.

"What are you exactly referring to, Mr. Whitmore?" Oliver Silverman asked with a trembling voice, pointing to himself.

"Were you at Sylvan's Valley Park two afternoons ago?"

"I don't travel such distances. It's too far for my limited mobility."

"The police showed me videos of you walking in the park at the exact time."

"And how did the police know it was this old man?" Oliver Silverman asked, his voice quivering, pointing to himself.

"Well, actually, I identified you. By your way of walking."

Anne listened to Michael's argument in astonishment, her brow furrowed. She felt deceived. "By his way of walking?" she silently exclaimed.

She interrupted the conversation with Oliver and confronted Michael.

"Really, Mike? I thought you had evidence from the police. You know perfectly well that two people can walk similarly, even identically. Remember it was one of your arguments in the plot of *Three Widows*?" She paused. Michael didn't respond, only nodded, and she continued. "You know that the process of walking involves a set of mechanical movements that are common to all human beings. The possibility of two people having a similar way of walking is very, very high. And using that argument with poor Oliver Silverman seems childish and out of place."

"Oliver, I beg you to forgive me. Anne is absolutely right. We've had a misfortune, and I thought..."

"You don't have to apologize. We all make mistakes throughout our lives. Who hasn't made a mistake at some point?" he tried to settle the matter, invited them inside, and asked Anne. "What was stolen from you, Miss Harrington?"

"A lot of money, Oliver, a tremendous amount of money. If I had it here right now, I would give it to you, believe me." Anne confessed him. She was consumed by guilt. She felt so ashamed that she avoided looking directly at him.

"Don't worry about it." he patted her arm. "I don't need money anymore, my dear. Would you like some tea? While the water is heating up, I'll tell you the news..."

When they left Silverman's apartment, Anne was truly furious with Michael.

"What the hell is wrong with you, Mike? You seem like a different person. How could you venture that it might be Oliver? You should have real evidence before barging into his home and yelling at him."

"I almost believe it was him, Anne. Too similar, and I don't know. It gives me a bad feeling. Besides, I think he's a bit crazy," he said, pointing to his temple with his finger. "So obsessed with the neighbours and he talks to Adeline's ghost."

"How dare you speak like that after murdering his wife? Of course! You can't put yourself in his shoes! The truth is, you disappoint me, Mike. I expected a bit more empathy from someone who has been suffering his whole life because of us."

"I can't think of a way to help him. If we confess and get locked up, how would that improve his situation? Would he regain his youth? Would Adeline come back?"

"No. None of that. He would feel that justice has been served, and he would find comfort for his soul, and maybe he would let Adeline rest in peace. I think I'm going to confess what happened."

Michael stopped on the sidewalk, a few meters away from the car parked on Evergreen Lane.

"Are you crazy, right? I don't think you're going to confess anything. I don't want to disrupt my life right now. The past is in the past. If you want, we can compensate him, as you say. But don't drag me into it!" he growled.

Anne looked at him with pity. Mike was spiralling down. His values were crumbling with age, and he was stuck. She believed that her presence in Sylvanville would help him bounce back by giving him love and advice. Anne hoped to improve his self-esteem and provide him with a path to resume writing, his great passion.

Anne was convinced that her friend was a skilful writer and she thought that, after the-stepping-stone-to-fame *Three Widows*, he would have to keep publishing, even if the conditions of the publishing house were not ideal, perhaps later on.

She didn't say anything. They continued walking to the car in silence. He dropped her off at the apartment building, and they bid each other farewell coldly.

Anne was terrified of the past, but she also knew that she could assume the blame and pay for it.

However, Michael Whitmore was wounded, and a rage grew within him as he made his way back home.

XXVII

The next day, the local newspaper reported another homicide. A huge headline on the front page wondered if Evergreen had been cursed: "ANOTHER MURDER ON EVERGREEN LANE RAISES NEW QUESTIONS. A young man stabbed in the back dies on the way to the hospital. The police, with no suspects, have several lines of investigation open..."

The continuous incidents on Evergreen Street had the neighbours concerned. The value of their homes was plummeting unless measures were taken to stop police cars from coming almost daily.

It was already the fourth time in a short period. And once again, Hilda Watson's house was the protagonist. The neighbourhood association met and proposed to protest at the town hall, demanding 24-hour surveillance until the deaths were clarified.

Silverman witnessed the scene from his window. "There's a lack of evidence," he repeated to himself, although he had a way to provide it. He cut out the information from that morning's press and placed it in a transparent sleeve. He stored it in the desk drawer alongside the others.

"Miss Harrington will have her story, Adeline. And it will be a good one."

He picked up the mobile phone from the nightstand. He wrote a message and sent it. He connected it to the charger, lay down facing the large window, and covered himself up.

XXVIII

The mobile phone vibrated and then started ringing. Michael sat up, looked at the screen, and answered.

"Mr. Whitmore, it's Chief Parker. I have news."

"I'm glad, Chief. What is it about?"

"You were right. The person appearing in the park video is Mr. Silverman."

Michael held his breath. He felt like shouting "bastard, son of a bitch" at that moment, but he restrained himself and asked Chief Parker:

"How did you find out?"

"You won't believe it. It was Oliver Silverman himself who contacted the office."

"Silverman himself!?" he exclaimed, even more astonished.

"Furthermore, he asked us to call you immediately and convey the news," Parker revealed.

"And did he give any reason for it?"

"Apparently, he explained that you informed him the bag stuff with your belongings, and he found one that could belong to you, but he wanted to confirm with the police in case it was another lost bag. When he described it to us, we assured him that it was undoubtedly yours, and he asked us to let you know so that it would be 'more official,' he said." Parker paused and then asked:

"Is it true that you're friends? Were you at his house yesterday?"

Silverman's account was not only convincing, but it was also surrounded by truth, in such a way that the chief's questions would confirm Oliver's alibi. There was no other possibility but to affirm both statements: "we are friends, and I was at his house talking about the case." Without a doubt, the old man had moved the pieces masterfully. "That Silverman is good. Very good," he thought to himself, but he didn't say anything else to the police chief. He didn't mention Silverman repeated ha hadn't been to the park. Silverman was lying. "Why was he fucking lying?", he thought angrily.

"Is it true, Mr. Whitmore?" Parker asked again and snapped him out of his reverie.

"I believe so. It's possible that it was my oversight, and it's true that we know each other. At first... uh!... I had a different impression, and to be honest, I apologize for the commotion I caused that day."

"Don't worry, it's completely understandable. If the bag contains what he declared, it's normal to feel that way."

"Yes. It was an impulsive and childish reaction on my part. But just thinking about having to renew my ID, request new cards... Imagine how much bureaucracy."

"I completely agree with you. Administrative procedures still need to be streamlined," he affirmed. "Is there anything else you need?"

"No, no, no. I'm eternally grateful, Mr. Parker, and please convey my gratitude to your team. The citizens of Sylvanville are at ease thanks to your work."

"I will relay your appreciation. Have a good day."

Michael said goodbye and jumped out of bed. He dressed in the same clothes as the day before and got into his car.

He drove fast, cutting through intersections and making sharp turns, as if he were a teenager. He accelerated a little beyond the allowed limit to reach Evergreen as soon as possible, climb the stairs to Oliver Silverman's apartment, and settle the pending matter from thirty years ago once and for all.

He opened the glove compartment and checked that the Glock was there. He was going to give the old man a good scare, and of course, he hoped he had the half-million ready to be returned.

"I will attack with all the pieces on the board, Silverman. With all of them," he silently brooded.

He didn't bother to park correctly. He got out of the car with the weapon hidden in his waistband. Two beeps confirmed that the car had locked. He didn't look back as he usually did when leaving the car on the street. He strode along the sidewalk and He pressed Silverman's intercom button several times.

The buzz of the latch sounded, and Michael pushed the door, climbed the stairs in strides, and when he was about to knock on the door, he didn't expect her to open it.

He couldn't believe it!

XXIX

"Anne?! What the hell are you doing here?" he exclaimed stunned. He looked over his shoulder, and behind her Oliver Silverman was standing with his thin, good-natured face and that complacent smile with which he always had greeted him.

He remained at the door for a moment, confused and bewildered. He couldn't process the fact that the "queen", the main piece of his side, was on the other side of the board.

Anne waited for Michael to assimilate the scenario and replied in a distant but calm voice, "Mr. Silverman has summoned us to this meeting, Michael. I think it's time to clarify things."

She discreetly checked that the Glock was secured and hidden beneath her jacket.

"Please, Mr. Whitmore, come in and have a seat. Let me know if you'd like something to drink."

The invitation seemed out of place and only increased his confusion and mistrust due to the unknown and unpredictable nature of this encounter. Whitmore was a writer who controlled his characters which he has always guided them with mastery, like puppets in a theatre crafted by himself, and he enjoyed playing with them and taking them to unimaginable extremes for the reader's pleasure. Somehow, he felt just as manipulated. It seemed that Anne had made a move without his consent. Was she hiding something too?

And Silverman's call to the police? The report document he signed in the police station would probably be now in the paper shredder bin. There was something dark in Silverman's life. Did the trauma caused by the Adeline's loss in the accident transform him into a resentful and unforgiving monster disguised as an innocent lamb? Furthermore… Was he Evergreen Lane murderer?!

He became defensive and walked backward, keeping a safe distance from Silverman and looking around as if expecting Adeline's ghost to appear.

"Mike, calm down, please. Let's talk and clarify things. I'm sure we'll all benefit from this conversation."

"Anne, that man is dangerous," he said to her slowly as if Silverman wasn't in the room. "He's been playing with us since the day we met at Sylvan's Corner."

"More or less, Mr. Whitmore. It's time for us to be honest, don't you think?" Silverman added, positioning himself beside Anne. Then he asked, "Why did you send the messages to Miss Harrington?"

Michael listened in astonishment. He looked at both of them, as the audience would in a tennis match.

"He's manipulating you, Anne! I didn't send any messages to your phone. I'm sure it was him, and he probably has something to do with Hilda's disappearance and the two widows."

"Now it's three, Mr. Whitmore. How curious that three widows are the protagonists of this non-fiction sequel. But believe me, it's mere coincidence. I assure you, it's mere coincidence," Mr. Silverman affirmed convincingly.

"Of course, Oliver, of course. And you'd also tell me that the encounter at Sylvan's Corner was a coincidence and that your calls to gather in this house were unintentional, and that the theft of the bag with half a million dollars has nothing to do with all of this," Michael listed and turned to Anne. "What more evidence do you want? Oliver wants revenge on us for what happened..."

"I never harboured the idea of seeking revenge, Mr. Whitmore. Nothing would bring Adeline back," he interrupted him.

"At least you admit that she's dead. It's a step forward," Michael continued with his arms crossed. "Because every time we've met, you always speak of her as if she were alive. Are you deranged, Silverman? Do you need some kind of treatment?"

"And who isn't deranged, Mr. Whitmore. But it's better if we move to the living room. My back starts to ache when I stand for too long.2

"Calm down, Mike. Oliver doesn't want to harm us. It has never been his intention to ruin our careers. I've been talking with him for a couple of hours, and I trust his word," Anne intervened.

"A couple of hours?!" Michael exclaimed, once again bewildered. "Since when did you switch sides? So, you've been plotting this encounter and you believe in an old madman capable of pushing us into the abyss..."

"Mr. Whitmore," Silverman interrupted again as he took a seat. "Allow me to repeat the question. Why did you send those unsettling messages to your best friend? Remember that Anne loves you, and you love her. According to Miss Harrington's account, you two never married, waiting for the opportunity to reunite." Michael stared at her open-mouthed. That idea had crossed both of their minds, but they had never made such a commitment. He felt that Anne had said too much and exposed him behind his back, as he was unaware of how much information Silverman had about his past...

"What's going on, Anne? Have you handed our opponent a manual with all our moves?" he reproached her, he was irritated.

"No, Mike. Please try to calm down. I'm willing to forgive you and love you as it has always been. And, furthermore, if you need half a million dollars, I'm willing to lend it to you."

"What kind of bullshit lie did he tell you?"

"Why don't you answer my question, Mr. Whitmore?" Silverman insisted in a relaxed tone. "Or would you prefer me to answer for you?"

"He means he wants to lie on my behalf," he said angrily. "Go ahead, Anne, and you know that I love fiction. This whole conversation, this whole story will be perfect for my next novel. Proceed."

"Alright. You made those threats because you're bankrupt," Anne observed Michael's changing expression. Oliver Silverman had touched a sensitive chord in his friend. She knew him better than her own mother after years of intimate confessions. She was certain that Silverman's words were accurate and had reached the part of the brain where emotions cannot be controlled.

"And how did you come to that conclusion? Make it easy for me to close the next chapter."

"Very well. I'll give you the long answer so you can choose what suits your character's dialogue. Take note."

Oliver Silverman had eighty years of life experience, although his somewhat frail appearance, thinness, and slightly hunched back due to age made him look even older. He had lived a lot. His green eyes, marked by deep wrinkles, exuded the wisdom that age had bestowed upon him.

That day he was wearing a dark grey suit with a matching tie and a white shirt underneath. Despite his advanced age and appearance, Oliver remained in good physical shape, and the electric cart story was a comfortable way to do the shopping and cover long distances, as he had explained to Anne before Michael's arrival.

He was a convincing person due to his calm and reflective attitude, and Anne had already noticed that he pondered things before speaking. With a soft and measured voice that denoted that wisdom and experience, he began to explain how a mobile phone could be cloned...

XXX

"Mr. Whitmore," he began his explanation, "cloning a mobile phone involves creating an exact copy of the original device, including all data and settings, and using this copy to access the phone's information.

"You may think that an old man like me isn't skilful, right? I inform you my work has always been in computing," he said and paused. Michael looked at Anne with eyes of astonishment. "Another check?" he feared.

"Those were different times, indeed! But I retired late and have witnessed the rapid development of this technology," he pointed to the phone resting on the desk and continued his explanation:

"There are two ways to clone a phone. I chose to introduce malicious software." He paused and confessed, "And that's where the first day at Sylvan's Corner comes into play. You unintentionally handed me the phone. To be true, I snatched it while you were focused on helping me to the restroom," he admitted and added: "This way, comfortably seated at that desk," he pointed to the other side of the room, "I was able to attack and access the other phone you might have brought today."

Michael instinctively placed his hand on his chest and made sure that the mobile phone, hidden inside an inner pocket, was still in place. It was a reflexive act that Anne noticed. Silverman was glad that he had brought it and continued:

"That's how I gained access to the device's information, including its location, text messages, emails, and other communications. Once the malicious software is installed on the original phone, the attacker can obtain a copy of the data stored on it. And in that way, I discovered that I had unleashed the fear that gripped my poor Anne Harrington in order to steal a million dollars."

The well soundproofed room highlighted the silence that the three of them kept, as if time had frozen in that instant. Anne had teary eyes fixed on Michael and he couldn't hold her gaze. Oliver Silverman took advantage of that moment to repeat the question:

"Why did you send the messages to Miss Harrington?" asked he calmly.

"Why did you resort to that strategy, Mike? You know I would have helped you blindly. I would have put the Daily Beacon at your feet..." Anne stopped when she noticed that Michael's anger was escalating.

The writer's heart was pounding, and the blood rushed to his head and ears as his anger grew. He paced back and forth in the room, gripping his head. Anne was scared for the first time in her life with Mike; she had never seen that flushed face, laboured breathing, and tense body. Michael pulled out the gun he had brought concealed to confront the black king and spoke slowly and gravely.

"I felt so ashamed, Anne," he confessed, struggling to hold back the words. "You were always better than me, and I was jealous of you. I feel like a failed writer, a failed man. I'm useless. But I didn't send the final message," he swore in almost a whisper, trying to prevent Silverman from hearing. "It was Oliver!" he shouted and pointed the weapon at him. "Now I realize it with his confession! He saw the first message and got involved in the game. I regretted what I had done when I saw that the mysterious person was following our movements and I really wanted to unmask him, wanted to know how he had replaced me, who he was, why he was torturing us like this..." He paused, lowered his head, and lamented, "I failed, Anne!"

"But it's not true, Mike. Nobody considers you a looser. You are highly respected in Sylvanville, and your works are popular..."

Michael's voice rose as he expressed his frustration:

"Fuck popularity! I don't need popularity; I need the profits from my sales!" he cried out in despair. Tears streamed down his cheeks. He stood up from his seat and pointed at the black king. "Where's the damn money, Oliver?"

Anne let out a scream of true terror. Michael's anger took control of him in that moment.

"What are you doing, Michael? Please calm down!" she pleaded. Anne had witnessed Michael's transformation while sitting, but at that moment, she stood up in terror. The scene unfolded slowly.

"Give me my damn money, Oliver! Bring it right now, or I'll splatter your brains on your fucking window!" he threatened again, trembling as he pointed at Oliver Silverman, who remained impassive, seated in the chair. "You've ruined my life! Everything was going to be perfect. I would have invested that money and returned Anne's share with interest!" he said and turned to Anne. "Believe me, Anne. It wasn't supposed to happen like this. I'm on a roll again. I'm back at my computer, writing ten thousand words a day for the past four days. I have it all here," he pointed to his head with the Glock. "I'll finish the novel in just over a week. I just wanted to clear my mind, get rid of the creditors. I'm about to lose the shitty apartment where I live and the shitty car I bought. It was a matter of a few weeks, paying some bills, and entering Crimemaster with a draft of success. I would have paid you back all the money and double!"

"Mike. Everything you're saying is true. I believe you," Anne tried to calm him, though she was trembling and on the verge of losing consciousness. "Keep the half-million, and if you want, I'll give you another half-million. With that, you can pay off debts and build a future. I'll help you."

"The lovely and intelligent Anne Harrington, the smartest girl in school, the perfect woman, the best reporter in the country, comes to save me... Let's see how you solve this ending, clever girl. You've allied yourself with the enemy. Come on! Make a move!"

Incomprehensibly, Mike also aimed at Anne's chest. He was so out of control and distorted that she felt his features belonged to someone else, as if Mr. Hyde had suddenly awakened.

Anne hasn't been able to interpret the signals of the past few days. In seconds, she realized that Michael Whitmore had gone through a very difficult stage in his life.

Now she was aware and fear, which almost escaped from her mouth, gave way to compassion. She had never seen him sob like a misunderstood child. Mike had always been her guardian angel, the strong one on the team, the voice whose arguments convinced anyone. She didn't understand what had happened and why he had awakened a ghost that was already buried to solve his present. She would have helped him however she could, financially or by putting the Daily Beacon at his service. His articles were read by hundreds of thousands of people across the country. She wanted to explain and try to calm him, but the sound of the doorbell and a voice from the other side stopped her.

"Sylvanville Police! Open the door, please."

XXXI

Michael looked out of the window. There were two police cars parked outside the building and two officers were guarding the main gate, so he suspected that two more were on the other side of Oliver's apartment door.

"Who the hell called the police?" Michael asked, enraged. "Was it you, old man? Huh? I'm sure it was you," he threatened with the gun and placed himself behind him. "Anne, open the door for the police," he demanded. "You'll see, sweetheart, I'll convince them to arrest this bastard for cloning a phone without my authorization, for spying on the neighbours, for stealing half a million dollars, for murdering," he told Anne and then shouted at Silverman, "I have connections in the town hall, Mr. Silverman! You won't get away with this!"

"Calm down, Mike. I'll open the door and they will handle the situation," she pleaded. "But put the gun away. Mr. Silverman isn't dangerous, he can't harm you. Please, calm down and I'll open..."

"Open the damn door!" he shouted in desperation.

The police officers entered with their guns drawn and aimed at him.

"Michael Whitmore, put your weapon down, please," the one who was in front of them instructed and repeated several times. "Look, I'll holster mine. Let's talk. Okay?"

"Okay," Michael muttered, calmer. He removed the gun from Oliver's head and relaxed the arm holding the weapon. In a quiet voice, he continued: "I want to report Mr. Oliver Silverman. He is a false and manipulative citizen who has been blackmailing us for almost two weeks, claiming that Miss Harrington and I were responsible for the accident that caused the death of his wife in 1993. A fact he can't prove, yet he has harassed us daily, threatened us, and extorted us. Furthermore, he spies on the neighbours. You can also add that he stole half a million dollars from Miss Anne Harrington and just admitted to fraudulently accessing my mobile phone to commit his crimes and manipulate everything to make it look like I'm the culprit. And I think he is the Evergreen Lane's murderer. He has violated numerous federal laws, officer."

"Alright, we believe you. Can you please facilitate the arrest? I would kindly ask you to place your weapon on the floor and step away from the suspect, so we can proceed to handcuff him," the officer had approached slowly as Michael listed the charges.

"Yes, of course, officer. I have always cooperated with the police," he slowly placed the gun on the floor, and the officer pounced on him, threw him to the ground, and restrained him with his knee on his back. The other officer also pounced on him and handcuffed him, while Michael struggled and shouted, "You're mistaken!" he repeated, yelling. "It's him, Oliver Silverman!"

"Mr. Whitmore, you are under arrest. You have the right to remain silent. Anything you say can and will be used against you in a court of law. You have the right to an attorney. If you cannot afford one, one will be provided for you," the officer raised his voice over Michael's. "If you wish to speak to an attorney before answering any questions, you have the right to do so! Do you understand the rights I just said to you?"

"Anne! Anne! What are they doing? It's not me! Anne, tell them they've got the wrong man, please."

Anne Harrington was crying bitterly, huddled in Mr. Silverman's armchair like a terrified child, unable to utter a word.

He couldn't look at him as they carried him away.

XXXII

Anne took long, deep breaths while Oliver tried to console her. She left the bag of money on the kitchen table. She made a comforting tea for herself, brought it over, sat beside her, and took her hand.

"I'm so sorry for the loss of Adeline," she said, sobbing. "How can I make it up to you?"

"You don't remember much of that fateful day, do you?"

"Yes, I do remember. You were trapped in the burning car, and your wife was calling for help."

"No, it didn't happen that way. I was outside the car. I tried to get her out of the flames, but I got caught," he pointed to his back. "I rolled on the ground. Adeline was unconscious, but her heart was still beating. It was the smoke that suffocated her and the fire that consumed her, but that part you didn't get to see. Mr. Whitmore didn't get out immediately. You were in shock, with your eyes fixed on the scene but absent, just like a moment ago. You froze due to the stress caused by the horrific scene of that fateful day, and you couldn't react. He didn't respond to my pleas. I held onto his arm and begged him not to leave. He pushed me away, got in the car, reversed, and sped away as if he had seen the devil."

Oliver stopped and looked up at the ceiling: "Somehow, it was hell: the smell of burning flesh is imprinted in my memory."

Tears welled up in his deep eyes, and he explained: "My poor Adeline burned, and I cried and screamed, alone and powerless. I knelt down and prayed to God to help her transition from this life to the next, and I promised her that she would live on within me. I didn't want to forget, and..." He paused, composed his voice, and finished the sentence, "Since then, Adeline has never lacked anything." He wiped away his tears, looked at Anne, and smiled. "I have never stopped sending her a message from my phone. I write to her every day because the signal travels through the sky, doesn't it? They say it goes from one satellite to another, and I'm sure she reads them."

Anne sobbed inconsolably as she listened to Oliver Silverman's tragic account of the horrible day. There was a silence, and she was finally able to speak.

"That scene is my nightmare, Oliver. Years of therapy haven't erased it. I still see the fire, as if the moment were happening in slow motion, and I feel tied to the car seat, unable to move, as if someone is holding me tightly. It's a recurring nightmare that I can't get rid of," she said between sobs. "I feel guilty. I wish we hadn't gone to that damn lookout that night. I had a literature exam the next day; I should have stayed, but Mike convinced me, and I never said no to him."

"Adeline and I hold no resentment, my dear Anne Harrington. Besides, we always read your articles because you represent this city to the whole world. We also admire Mr. Whitmore. I have all his novels, and we will cherish the signature in the copy of *Three Widows*."

"I think you're lying to comfort me, aren't you?" Oliver's calm voice had a reassuring effect on her; she had calmed down. She was no longer trembling. She looked at him and squeezed the wrinkled hand that held hers.

"You know what my favourite author says: 'Reality overcomes fiction'. And we're going to stick with that phrase. Agreed? I admire you, Miss Harrington, and I'm going to provide you with the information for the best report of your life," he smiled. "Well, it's an exaggeration, of course. But it could be," he said in a honeyed and consoling voice, and added: "Would you like to hear the story of the three widows who died on Evergreen Lane? I know it from beginning to end," he confessed.

Anne felt intrigued by the idea, but she was overcome with sorrow for Michael's situation.

"What will happen to Mike?" she asked.

"I won't press charges. Don't worry. My account will be his next novel. And I would be so thrilled to be the protagonist! I think he'll title it *The Murders of Evergreen*. At least you could suggest the idea, don't you think?" he said.

"Well, I do. I'll convey your proposal and report everything you reveal to me," Anne replied.

"Then, are you ready?" Oliver asked with sparkling eyes.

"Of course. I have the soul of a reporter," she smiled.

"I know it. Make yourself comfortable and take out your recorder."

XXXIII

The complexity of the events on Evergreen Lane had baffled the police. Four murders in a short period of time. Hilda Watson's house seemed to be cursed or possessed by demons, as the evidence was never conclusive. The criminologists had the police station's whiteboard filled with photos, erased lines, and question marks on each of the fact-finding leads they had noted down: jealousy, inheritances, ambitions, strained relationships, a squatter, drugs... The list was endless, but nothing seemed to have a solid foundation that would connect those dots or lead anywhere.

The neighbours, genuinely concerned and shocked, staged a protest in Washington Square in front of the Town Hall, demanding extraordinary security measures, including the installation of more cameras. It seemed like a dark cloud was hanging over Evergreen, and for a long time, no one trusted anyone. The days of neighbours exchanging pastries and lavishly decorating their houses to celebrate Halloween and Christmas might never be repeated.

For a few weeks, Oliver observed from his window security company vehicles installing new alarms-

advanced systems that offered 24-hour surveillance. Alternatively, they upgraded the existing systems with more sophisticated ones, featuring early warning alerts or connections to the local police.

Despite having almost certainty that the young squatter was responsible for the murders, something didn't add up for the detectives in Sylvanville. The uncertainty and lack of resolution led some homeowners to put their houses up for sale at outrageous prices, far from the effort it took to acquire or build them. They preferred to continue their lives elsewhere, away from the sinister atmosphere.

Other neighbours reported sleeping poorly and resorted to medication to correct their sleep deficits and try to carry on with their lives... Except for Oliver Silverman.

One morning, when the street was no longer the centre of attention, he woke up early. He prepared toast, a cup of coffee with milk, and set the table for Adeline as well. He turned on the TV:

"The Evergreen murder case has been solved. The police have found compelling evidence in Hilda Watson's house that places the two young suspects at the crime scene. It includes an article of clothing soaked in the victim's blood and mud from the area where she was fatally attacked, according to forensic laboratory analyses. A crucial lead that went unnoticed in the initial records inexplicably..."

Silverman listened attentively to the news as he chewed and sipped his coffee. He smiled with satisfaction and was glad to hear the good news. His mobile phone's ringtone distracted him.

"Oliver Silverman speaking, can I help you?" he said.

"Mr. Silverman, this is Brian O'Connor from Elite Notary Services," the person on the other end of the line informed him. "According to the documents and instructions we have, Mrs. Hilda named you as the sole heir."

"Are you sure it's me, Mr. O'Connor?" he asked perplexed.

"Yes. We have the inheritance document with the justifications for her decision. Mrs. Watson held you in high regard. She deeply regretted the sadness that had consumed your life after the loss of your wife in a terrible accident. Since she had no direct heirs, she decided to leave the house, all its contents, and savings in your name, stating that you took care of her and provided companionship for a long time."

"Well, well. How kind of Mrs. Watson. Hilda was like a sister to me," he admitted, "but I never imagined..."

"It's karma, people say, Mr. Silverman. You reap what you sow, or something like that. Anyway, whenever you can, please come to our office to receive the documentation and settle the assets."

"Why haven't I been notified earlier?" Silverman inquired.

"We can't do so if there's an ongoing investigation. Until the case is resolved, the documentation must remain in our custody unless a judge orders us to provide information."

"And the police didn't ask you?"

"Of course, they did. They asked if either of the two suspects were heirs. Obviously, we answered no. But the law doesn't oblige us to disclose that someone else is named in the will unless a judge requests it," he repeated.

The old man thanked him with a tremulous voice and showered praises when referring to poor Hilda. He said his goodbyes and hung up. He finished his coffee calmly.

He picked up his mobile phone and wrote a message to his eternal wife: "It took me a little longer, Adeline," he spoke aloud as he typed. "That damn squatter messed up my plans when I had already taken care of Hilda, and to top it off, he rented a bedroom. I took care of that too! And Mr. Whitmore has paid for his guilt. Don't you think so, Adeline? I miss you so much."

He pressed the send icon and placed the phone on the night bed table. He tore out the pages from the notebook containing his observations and let the fire turn them into ashes in the metal wastebasket. He got up swiftly, humming *One Way or Another* by Blondie.

He looked at himself in the mirror one last time. He wanted to make sure his tie wasn't crooked; it irritated Adeline, especially when he had important interviews, like on that occasion.

Before leaving the apartment, he pointed the telescope towards the number 24 on Evergreen Lane. Mr. Brownsworth had been in the hospital for three weeks, and in an informal conversation, Eleanor Brownsworth, a retired teacher, sadly explained the frailty of her husband's health.

"Another vulnerable widow in the neighbourhood, Adeline?" he sent the question to his wife. and typed again: "Are you sure she didn't poison our neighbour? Because in such a case she would have to atone for her worldly sins too, don't you think?"

He waited for a moment and then wrote, "Yes, Adeline. You're right, it's time to sell everything and move to a peaceful island with better weather for our bones. I love you so much."

He sent the last message.

THE END

San Cristóbal de la Laguna, 7th May 2023